I0619133

PETER GIGLIO
STEALING NIGHT

Stealing Night
Copyright © 2013 by Peter Giglio

ISBN: **1938644093**

ISBN-13: **978-1-938644-09-2**

First Edition
April 2013
Nightscape Press, LLP
www.nightscapepress.com

Edited by Robert S. Wilson
Cover art by Gary McCluskey

Printed in the United States of America and the United Kingdom

10 9 8 7 6 5 4 3 2 1

Advance Praise for *Stealing Night*

"With razor-sharp characterization and hard-as-nails prose, Peter Giglio's *Stealing Night* is a literary punch in the gut—brutal, stunning, and not to be missed."
—**Tim Waggoner**,
author of *Like Death* and *The Harmony Society*

"Sunfall is one hell of a place. And Peter Giglio is one hell of a writer. I am impressed, not only with Giglio's fine prose and appropriate poetic moments, but also by the tension he builds throughout the story. Gripping, endearing and suspenseful, *Stealing Night* is a wonderful book."
—**Benjamin Kane Ethridge**,
Bram Stoker Award-winning author of
Black & Orange and *Bottled Abyss*

"An agonizingly deep look into loss and rebuilding, bad decisions and their immutable consequences, Peter Giglio's *Stealing Night* is an indispensable piece of painfully human crime fiction. It will tear your heart out and you'll thank him for it."
—**Ed Kurtz**,
author of *A Wind of Knives* and *Dead Trash*

"*Stealing Night* masterfully weaves themes of humanity and sacrifice into a story of love, life, and redemption. Peter Giglio's compelling thriller will keep you captivated until the very end!"
—**Rena Mason**,
author of *The Evolutionist*

"This is the kind of story relevant to today's America; its pulse beats strong, the blood inside derived from its heirs, but unmistakably young, fresh, and vital. Giglio leads a new pack of modern noir voices, and this is not a story I'll forget."

—**John Palisano**,
author of *Nerves* and *Bipolar Express*

"Mr. Giglio's ear for dialogue might very well have been scalped cleanly off Elmore Leonard's head. Someone should check. Yes, the players here are that good! *Stealing Night* is smart, effectively rural in its sensibilities, and most certainly a winner!"

—**Jon Michael Kelley**,
author of *Seraphim*

"Layered, haunting and elegantly written, Peter Giglio's rural crime thriller *Stealing Night* rushes at you like a pair of headlights on a dark and lonely road, leaving you shaken and awed by the story's raw power of love & redemption."

—**Jan Kozlowski**,
author of *Die, You Bastard! Die!*

This book is dedicated to
Rick Hautala –
an inspiration in my formative years and a good friend later.
Heaven better have great cigars.

In a murderous time
the heart breaks and breaks
and lives by breaking.
It is necessary to go through
dark and deeper dark
and not to turn.

—Stanley Kunitz,
The Testing Tree

I'm taking a ride
with my best friend.
I hope he never lets me down again.

—Depeche Mode,
Never Let Me Down

PROLOGUE

On a cold Saturday morning in late March, I woke up.

With Nora's head nuzzling my chest and the day's first light bleeding through the bent and broken blinds of my tumbledown living room, I studied the rise and fall of her breathing.

There she was, my eleven-year-old niece.

No one ever needed me before, and guardianship sure as hell was never a thing I went in search of. That doesn't change the way things work. Charges, whether we seek them or not, have a way of finding us in those dimly lit, cold moments of our lives.

My nameless cat caught my attention with a loud yelp, pulling me away from the cadence of Nora's fragile existence. In her paws was a half-eaten rat. In her eyes, satisfaction, as if she were saying, *Caught another one, Daddy. Aren't you proud of me?*

Pride, however, was not my thing. The gateway drug, as I saw it, to everything I never wanted to be.

A group of large wild cats is called a pride. Those fuckers'll rip your head off.

Put a bunch of housecats in the same space and the worst thing you're likely to get is a mess. That aside, I'd always admired feline independence. Let's face it, they don't need us. Never have. What they need is something to fuel their predacious energies and curiosities, and I was the perfect cat owner, living in a two hundred dollar a month shithole with rodents aplenty.

Now Nora needed me, and I was starting to understand big cats.

March was when her mother, my sister, really started going off the rails. Lily had been broken for a long time, but not to the degree that caring for her child wasn't priority number one. Things, as things have a way of doing, had changed, and that morning was the dawn of my niece's first sleep over at "Uncle Jack's." The morning I discovered a deep love for another human being; the morning I started seeking higher ground.

Like I said, I woke up.

I hadn't slept a wink the night before.

TUESDAY

CHAPTER ONE

A panting mutt slogs next to me and stops. It looks miserable in this heat—looks the way I feel—but I keep scrubbing the rims of a 2004 Acura, trying to ignore the animal, who's just standing in front of Bud Sweeny's Auto World, looking at me.

"Move on," I growl. And the dog, it moves on. Was a time when I might have felt sorry for the thing, given it a scrap of food, maybe even taken it in.

Maybe not. This one looks sick.

My cat came down with a light sneeze last month. She died.

On my knees, I'm done with disease.

Back to work.

Getting the grime off these cars isn't easy. First of all, Bud's fleet is made up of revitalized relics beyond their intended expiration. The wind makes everything worse. Anyone who thinks of wind as a blessing on a hot day—a nice cool breeze, perhaps—lives in lands with large bodies of water and mountains. Someplace nice. Insult added to injury, our nosebleed winters make summers all the more ironic. This land is manic.

The flatland wind, she's fierce today, hot and gritty, as unforgiving to flesh as metal. Next door, the Dairy Queen sign rattles. Across the street, First Confederated Bank's yellow banner, proclaiming *Lowest Interest Rates Ever,* flaps violently and looks like it might sail Ozward any moment.

"Somewhere, over the rainbow..."

I open the valve of the hose and spray the wheels. Even the water's hot, and the occasional backsplash does nothing to relieve the sickness deep in my head and heart and gut.

I said I'm done with disease, not that it's done with me.

"Hey Jack," Bud bellows, drawing my attention away from matters at hand.

I shut off the hose. "Afternoon, Bud."

"Do you have a minute to talk?" he asks.

You'd think Bud might invite me into his air-conditioned office for such discourse, but that's not his way. He wipes his brow with a handkerchief, even though he's been outside for less than a minute. A stuffed pig in a cheap suit, and when he's done talking, he'll amble back into his Freon cocoon and forget all about me.

"I appreciate what you're trying to do, son," he says.

"I'm just trying to wash these —"

"C'mon, Jack, don't play dumb. Stuart Mills just phoned. Told me all about your pitch."

So this is what's on Bud's mind. Was only a matter of time, I guess. Was hoping we could have this conversation when I'd gained a stronger hand, but here I go. I take a deep breath, then say, "What's wrong with trying to drum

up some business for the lot, Bud? Just trying to prove that
I—"

"Stuart wasn't so happy."

"Told me he was in the market for a car. His daughter,
Emily, just turned sixteen and—"

"Folks 'round here like to talk, Jack. They got nothing
better to do. But Stuart's been out of work for two months.
Didn't appreciate the hard sell, the guilt approach."

I'd laid it on too thick and had known it even in the
moment. What could I do? It was the closest I'd come to
success, and I couldn't just give in, back down. Stuart
promised he wouldn't say anything to Bud, but I should
have fucking known better. Bud's right; people around
here, they do like to talk.

"I'm sorry," I say. "I don't have any experience, any
training. Maybe you could teach me—"

"Here's the thing, kid, I'm less than a year from
retirement. Time has been kind to me, more or less." Bud
pats his gut and forces a lopsided smile. "Now..." He
shakes his head, looks around with more than a trace of
disgust. "Town's dried up. I sell two, maybe three cars a
month, and that's...well, that's enough for me—got a lot of
steaks in the freezer, if you know what I mean."

"Yeah, but it could be better. I'll work in the office. You
got that empty desk in there. I'll help you go out on top,
blaze of glory shit, like it should be. We can move the rest
of your inventory. What do you have to lose?"

Bud laughs. "I'll move the rest of the fleet in one
transaction. Already have a buyer, a clearinghouse in
Omaha. Not much of a profit, mind you, but... Look, I
understand what you're trying to do."

I doubt he really grasps my intentions, but I nod agreement.

"You want to take the lot over when I give her up," Bud says, "but you have to understand, the car business isn't what she used to be. And being a used car salesman?" A dry chuckle. "There's not exactly a lot of glory in the profession. Never was."

"You don't understand, Bud. I'm just trying to make enough money to get out of this place. Like I've told you before, washing cars two days a week for minimum wage isn't cutting it."

Bud shrugs then blows smoke at the sky. "I'd do more for you if I could, but I don't need a salesman. This has always been a one man operation, and I've never, will never, take my pitch door-to-door." His stare locks into my gaze. "People," he says, "don't appreciate the *Watchtower* approach. Damn Jehovah's Witnesses ruined the whole knock-and-shake racquet long ago. Truth is, salesmen didn't do such a hot job with the whole business, either."

"Bud, I'm hungry. I'll hustle. I'll work on commissions. All I need is a phone and—"

"No," Bud groans, shaking his head. "I've been good to you. You come my way a few months back looking for work. I tell you I don't have anything, but you don't go away. So what do I do? I set you up with this job washing cars. Not much, but more than I need or can afford."

"Thanks. I do appreciate that. But what's wrong with—"

"I don't mean to be an asshole, Jack. You're good people. Really. If there was one person in this town I could help, it'd be you, but there's one way and only one way a guy my age does things, and that's *my way*. I've worked too hard for too long to let anyone, even a scrapper like you, call the shots. If you don't want what I've given you...?"

What can I say? What can I do? I can't lose my only income, so I apologize and go back to spraying the Acura.

Bud doesn't walk away immediately. "Why don't you go up to Henderson's Farm," he shouts over the sound of the high-power spray. "They're always looking for good men up there. Good pay, too. Long as you don't mind getting bloody, it's a fine bit of work."

Still spraying, I say, "Place is twenty miles west of here. Don't suppose you could set me up with a car? Weekly payment plan?"

Bud lights another cigarette and shakes his head. "Ten years ago, sure. I can't shoulder a loan no more—don't even plan to be doing this long enough to see it through. Don't guess the banks'd touch you?"

"You kidding?" I say with a joyless snort. "I can't even get a cell phone plan. Gotta buy prepaid minutes, most of them used shaking the trees for you." I'm trying to keep anger out of my tone but that's not working.

"Don't get bent out of shape with me. I never asked you to do that. Never wanted you to. So don't run that trip on me you ran on Mills. Doesn't become you anyhow. Makes a man look...weak."

I shut off the hose. "Bud, I know. None of this is your fault, okay? I'm just trying to get my family out of this hole."

Bud nods. "Can't say I blame you. Town's gone to shit."

"Sunfall's always been shit, and you know it. Maybe you didn't realize it because you were doing well enough.

We've got the Millie-Mart, the bank, the DQ, the coffee shop on Cedar, and your lot, and it sounds like we won't have that much longer."

"Or the DQ," Bud says.

Rumors had circulated, so I'm hardly surprised; still, I say, "Really?"

"Yeah, Mark Rollins's lease is up in October. Told me he's not renewing."

"I need four grand," I say, cutting to the chase. I could care less about Dilly Bars or Mark Rollins. "That's all I need."

"How much you have now?"

"Little more than five hundred."

"Can't do it for a little less? Make some sacrifices? Cut a few corners? I know a guy who owns some reasonable properties in Lincoln."

"That's not the way," I say. "Nora…she deserves a real home. And we all deserve a little opportunity. Lincoln's far better than here but not good enough, and it doesn't seem like a fun place to struggle."

Genuine sympathy sweeps Bud's face, a rare expression. "There's no fun place to struggle," he mutters, then wipes his forehead again, exhaling smoke with a dry cough. Stamping out the butt with his boot, he says, "Keep washing cars, Jack. Best I can do."

I walk back to my apartment, tired but not dead, eating a bargain burger from the DQ as I try to process Bud's words. He's a good guy, despite dressing me down earlier, and I know he'll do the right thing if I make a sale — cut me in on the money; maybe even give me the empty desk. There's really no other short-term way out of this place. Nothing else of value to sell in this town, no other way to make quick cash, and Bud knows it. For everything he said, he never came right out and told me to stop. Sure, I'm grasping at straws, but I'll take what I can get.

I've seen Bud's markup while snooping through his books when he's out to lunch. The margins are big. Twenty percent of five deals, which I know is fair, would get me — get us — out of here fast. Although I hate myself a little for invading a good man's privacy, I don't think I've gone too far. Not like I took anything that wasn't mine.

The same sad dog from earlier looks up at me from a prairie-yellow patch of yard. It doesn't even have the energy to wag its tail or whine. Black dog. A Labrador?

I kneel down in front of the animal as it scrambles painfully to its feet, then lay the rest of my burger on the ground.

The dog's still eating — slowly, as if this may be its last meal — when I turn and walk away.

CHAPTER TWO

When I get home, Ernie Sullivan's pounding on my door. He's my landlord and not a good guy like Bud. A vile vision, rather, decked out in a ratty Tasmanian Devil tee and cum-stained cargo shorts.

"Stop waking the dead," I say, "I'm right here."

His head swivels in my direction as he sneers. "Where've you been? You're two months behind on—"

"Work. Trying to earn what I owe."

"So you're telling me you don't have the money yet? Is that what you're trying to say?"

I smile and shrug. This guy doesn't scare me. He's got four vacant units, and my debt is better than a fifth goose egg. He knows I'm smart enough to realize this—at least that's what I think—and it's clearly getting under his flea-ridden flesh. "Times are tough, Ernie. What can I tell you?" For dramatic effect, I turn out my empty pockets, which seems to increase Ernie's anger. I don't generally like pissing people off, but the gambit feels right with this guy.

"Times are tough for me, too, Jack. All you people think you can slow-pay me like I'm the fucking government or something. This doesn't work that way. If you want a roof over your head, you've got to pay." He heaves a consumptive sigh, then adds, "Don't think I won't—"

"Please," I say, trying to look intimidated for his benefit, or is it mine? "I've been looking after my niece lately, picking up the slack for her mom. Haven't I always been on time in the past?"

"The past doesn't feed me. Besides, that's when you were on the dole. Now that you're working, I can't count on you."

"Trying to be an honest man. Not the easiest thing for a guy in my situation. Not these days."

"Hey, pal, I don't care where your money comes from, I just—"

"What's the problem here?" A voice booms behind us. I cringe, knowing immediately who it is.

Lee.

He jaunts toward us, the image of big-city slick ten years outdated: spiky blond hair, a black pinstripe shirt, perfectly pressed slacks. His face is adorned with the big toothy smile and wild eyes of a wolf.

"Hey, amigo," he says. Grabbing my hand, he pulls me into a half-hug then slaps me hard on the back. After a quick scowl at Ernie, he aims his frenzied focus back at me. "Who's this clown?" he growls in a whisper.

"I'm his landlord," Ernie says, taking an aggressive step at Lee. "Your friend here's two months behind on his rent."

"Look," I say, "can we talk about this later?"

Digging a hand into his pocket, Lee asks, "How much does my boy here owe?"

"Four hundred," Ernie snaps.

Lee laughs, big and rich and insincere as hell. "At least you don't overcharge for this dump."

Ernie doesn't look amused, and my ninety-nine cent dinner now feels like a ball of grease in my guts. Rolling, rolling, trying to break free.

My eyes widen as Lee whips out a wad of cash and peels off four one hundred dollar bills, and Ernie's displeasure fades, making room for a blooming, hideous smile—the brown rose of Nebraska. The scab snatches the cash from my old high school friend, then says, "You're foolish to bail this guy out, you know?" He points at me, like he's some kind of warden and I'm his prisoner. That dirty smile doesn't fade. "But thank you just the same."

"You got your money," Lee says in a low, even voice. Then he shouts, "Now get the fuck out of here!"

Ernie doesn't press his luck. He moves quickly for his car.

I look at Lee, gob smacked, struggling for words, and he stares through me.

"Been a long time, amigo," he says.

"Where've you been?"

"Omaha, St. Louis, Chicago. Bunch of places. Making contacts, laying down tracks, working on production deals. Almost signed with a major label, but my agent wouldn't let me touch the three-sixty Sony was offering."

I have no idea what he's talking about. Can't be music; fucker's tone deaf; couldn't even learn how to play "Mary Had a Little Lamb" on the saxophone without fouling every third note. Then again, the doggerel poetry of spitting rhymes doesn't require the embrasure of woodwind mastery. "That's cool," I say. "But, Lee...I don't know how I'm gonna repay—"

"You could start by inviting me in and offering me a beer."

I unlock the door, open it. "Come in," I say, already regretting it.

So here's Lee, strutting around the dump, holding court.

"...and then it was on to Chicago, where..."

Was really looking forward to my last beer after a long day, but now it's clutched in his hand, and I'm wishing I'd stopped off at the Millie-Mart for more; not that I should be spending what little money I have on such luxuries, but the errand might have changed my fortune in the guest department. Hindsight's a bitch.

"...some studio time, but not as much as..."

I'm tuning in and out, waiting for the babbling brook of Lee's mouth to tire.

"...met my agent in Gene Simmons's restaurant; you know, the guy from Kiss with the long tongue?"

"Gene Simmons is your agent?" I ask.

"No. Aren't you listening? We met at Gene's restaurant."

"Oh, was Gene there?"

"Are you fucking with me?"

I think yes, but say, "No, go on," and he does.

Lee rolls into my life every few months with a bunch of bullshit stories, rubbing my nose in his "success," his life beyond the shackles of Sunfall. Small mercy, he's always in like a lion, out like a lamb, tired and hung-over at the end of our time, promising a bunch of shit he can't deliver on, like, "I'll send you a plane ticket, bring you out to LA," or "We need you out in NYC." Fact is, I don't know where he lives or what he does, and I don't want to.

Part of me suspects that his real residence is still right here in Nowhere Nebraska, living low with the grandmother that raised him; that the space between these visits is all part of some illusion. Some…delusion. Dare I call bullshit? No. That'd only make matters worse. Best to let him have his moment, fuck with him in moderation, then move on.

Lee and I were tight back in school. We used to skip classes together, pass the same misguided girls back and forth, smoking copious pot we bought from some fuck at Sunfall Manor, before it burned to the ground, killing said fuck, the town's only dealer. I'm sure another fuck has filled the void, but I don't pay attention to these things anymore. Probably should, considering the condition my sister's in. But…

We were losers who had each other, which was enough in those days, even if we had nothing in common and I found him annoying.

The more I look back — something I try not to do — the more I realize Lee was much more than an annoyance. He was an obstacle. I had good grades, tested high in every subject, and could have made something of my life with a little focus. But I didn't do well enough to earn scholarships and grants, which was the only way I was ever going to college.

Mom, she kicked me flat on my ass a few weeks after my eighteenth birthday. Haven't talked to Dad since I was thirteen. Both of 'em made too much money for me to get student loans, and I didn't know shit about emancipation. So I have a lot of reasons to hate Lee, even though he just laid four Benjies on my rent. There are many good reasons to hate a lot of people. But I'm trying to keep anger in my rearview. It's like the Buddhists say: "Holding onto anger is like drinking poison and expecting the other person to die." That's some deep shit I read in a book, and it makes solid sense. Too bad it's like most things that are right—easier said than done. Buddha excels in that department, but the fat bastard would have made a lousy used car salesman.

"What about you, Jack? What's keeping you busy?" he asks. His eyes don't hide great expectations for small revelations.

"I've been taking care of my niece a lot."

"Lily's girl? Norma?"

"*Nora*," I spit, angry at myself for making her name sound ugly, accusatory, but I can't help my tone. The asshole before me is one of half a dozen clowns that might be her dad, and he can't even remember her name. I can't help but picture Maury Povich pulling out the results of a paternity test.

"*And the father is…*"

Trust me, that's one episode of daytime television I'd kill or die to prevent. Any chance of a link between Lee and Nora—well, that's a blood test that should forever go untaken.

"How's Lily doing?" he asks, pretending to care.

"She's a mess."

He shrugs, paces around some more, then says, "Well, it's a good thing she has a brother like you."

"I guess."

The sun's setting now, and silence settles over my living room. Lee, he's still pacing, looking deep in thought. Me, I'm just sitting on the dingy couch, hoping this means he's winding down. After several minutes of this empty pageant, I start getting twitchy. Lee's silence is always a cause for anxiety. Finally, I stand up and say, "It's been nice seeing you again."

His expression conveys hurt, like I've just pissed in his eyes and called it sunshine, but his mouth backs its shit down with, "I just got here," followed by a mischievous grin.

"I'm tired, Lee. I've been working—"

"Tired my ass."

"C'mon, man, I—"

"Dude, I barely ever come into town any more. Besides, I got some pills that'll give you a second wind."

"No. No pills." Last time I took pills Lee gave me, I didn't sleep for a week.

"What a pussy," he moans.

"All right. All right. What do you wanna do?" I hate myself for asking this, 'cause now I'm committed to whatever he says next. I mean, fuck, the guy just dropped four hundred bucks on my sorry ass. How the hell can I kick him out?

"I wanna go for a ride," he says.

CHAPTER THREE

There are worse things than a ride with Lee. If nothing else, the guy works his Mustang like Gosling in *Drive*. Not that his model is classic muscle. It's just made to look the part, like Lee himself. Still, I'll say this: the wild terrain we gamble is no stranger to him; he knows exactly how fast he can take each curve, each bend, and not a single M.P.H goes wasted.

Window down, hair blowing, I feel alive. Blood pumping. Heart racing. Along for the ride. Normally I'd hate the trip-hop that's thumping, hammering my chest and jaw, but the arrhythmic beats mix with the wild night wind and make a strange helter-skelter sense.

The yellow line of the two-lane zigs and zags, and a crimson moon punctuates the sky, hanging low and pregnant just shy of the flat horizon.

Lee downshifts, slows through a sharp turn. His hands are steady at ten and two, eyes trained with gravity that's rare, especially for him. Damn, I envy that kind of focus. That level of intensity. The whole thing's downright inspirational, despite how I feel about my friend in other terms.

The road straightens, and Lee slides the car back into sixth. The Mustang jumps, whipping my neck into the headrest and sending my stomach into my throat.

No sooner have we reached maximum velocity, I notice three deer galloping in a nearby field and point to them. Lee takes notice and slows the car. He might be a big city wanderer now, but he's still clearly in tune with the rural rules of the road.

Oncoming headlights approach. Fast. And my mind drifts.

When I was a kid, I was terrified at night by approaching cars on two lane highways. I'd spent a lot of time on back roads with my dad, a traveling salesman, and back then I'd frequently make my fears known.

"Don't be afraid," Dad would soothe. "They're just stealing night, messing with the way you see things. Trust me, they're not coming for us."

A deer splits from the pack, breaking roadward, coming into our path.

Lee brings the Mustang to a crawl, but the oncoming car...they don't see the wayward buck.

Lee honks his horn, flashes his high-beams, but the car keeps coming...coming...

"Fuck," Lee shouts, pulling over to the shoulder and killing the tunes. "Assholes are gonna get us killed!"

The deer's eyes glow gold in the headlights. With graceful, quick strides, it must think it can outrun anything. It's wrong, of course, dead wrong. This beautiful beast is a bullet from the gun of God.

Lee honks and flashes again, but deer and motorist charge on, the deer crossing into the road. I cringe and want to close my eyes but can't. Survival instincts kicking up dust, I open the door and rapidly distance myself from my would-be steel coffin, running...running...

Lee doesn't call for me, but he doesn't get out of the car, either. Like a ship's captain, he stays with his vessel, and I find myself uttering a silent prayer to a god I've never believed in. For Lee. For all of us.

The driver of the oncoming car must see the deer now, but it's too late. The night is alive with the squeal of breaks and tires as the car loses true and slides sideways in the high-beams of Lee's prized possession. The out-of-control vehicle, a compact coupe, broadsides the deer, which goes down with a dull *thwap* as rubber and road divorce.

Time seems to slow...

Dead still, my pulse thrumming into overdrive, I watch the car somersault, miss Lee's Mustang by a few feet, maybe less, then thud unceremoniously in the chigger-rich, weed-choked field, no more than twenty feet from me. The car's on its head, wheels spinning, smoke billowing.

"Fuck!" Lee shouts, now standing beside his ride. "Did you see that? Fucking thing almost took my head off!"

I race for the wreckage.

"Careful," Lee warns. "Thing might explode."

But I'm not listening to his shit. We've both seen too many movies, but Hollywood's a fucking liar, and I know how rare it is for wrecked cars to spontaneously combust. Lee, on the other hand, is the kinda guy who believes all the glossy lies we're sold routinely—the good, the bad, and the ugly.

"Call 911," I shout, "my phone's at home."

The passenger door of the wreck pops open, and a bloody girl staggers out.

"Are you okay?" I ask. "Are you—"

"Jason!" she cries. "Jason!"

"Is Jason the...?" I start, then a glimpse into the car reveals her driver. He's wrapped around the steering wheel, covered in blood, lifeless eyes wide, limbs akimbo. The girl stumbles, struggling to stay on her feet, clearly disoriented. And Jason, if that is the driver's name, is dead. Lee's walking around the car, peering into the windows, shaking his head.

I approach the girl, gently put my hands on her shoulders. The sharp scent of gasoline looms large, making me think that Lee's fears might be warranted after all.

Shhhuck, shhhuck, shhhuck.

I'm grinding my teeth, a nervous habit in times of stress. Taking a deep breath, I do my best to internalize my tremors, then say, "It's going to be all right. We're going to call for help," in an amazingly calm tone.

"Jason," she shouts. "Is he okay? Is he okay?"

Lee rounds the car, heading toward me and the girl, pulling something out of his pocket. His cell phone, I guess, but my focus is trained on her. "Listen," I say, "my friend is going to call 911, get an ambulance out here. Everything's going to be all right."

Shhhuck, shhhuck, shhhuck.

Dammit, my inner voice warns, *pull your shit together.*

She nods, tears streaming down her face. "Th-thank you," she manages. She's pretty with her plump, sunkissed cheeks—can't be more than eighteen or nineteen. My heart sinks for her. To lose someone so young, to —

"Back away from her," Lee growls.

"What?" I say. "Why?" I turn and look at my friend, who doesn't have a cell phone in his hand, and hope fades fast.

Lee levels the handgun at her head as I stumble backward. "No," I scream.

She doesn't even see it coming. With a blast of sound and fury, her head goes limp as she tumbles to the ground.

Lee stuffs the piece back in his slacks then turns and strides to the wrecked car.

"What the fuck?" I say, hardly able to believe what's happening.

Lee snaps the passenger seat forward and reaches into the back. "Shut up, Jack," he says. "This'll all make sense in a minute."

But he's wrong. Even if he pulls Hitler out of the backseat along with irrefutable documents linking these kids to the holocaust, the trigger moment will never make sense. He pulls a pink Hello Kitty backpack out of the car, drops it on the ground, then snatches a stack of money from it. Holds it up. "Saw this sticking out of the bag," he says with a grin. Then he bends down, unzips the bag the rest of the way, and his smile widens. He lifts the backpack and turns it so I can see what's inside.

It's filled with cash.

"Your troubles are over, amigo," Lee says.

CHAPTER FOUR

My troubles are far from over. I know this. Yet, I can wrap my mind around nothing as Lee drives us back to my apartment. Anger and fear are as distant as love and hope and as useless as hatred. I don't even have the energy to grind my teeth.

All that resonates is the girl's face, only a few years removed from Nora's—similar structure, the same green eyes shining in the darkness. Someone's daughter. Their charge.

Have mercy on the soul that fails the child, I think, and the darkening night blurs past in a nightmare mockery of time and space. Light dances in the periphery of my tear-glassed gaze, and a tidal wave din—engine racing, Lee wheedling, heart pounding, blood flowing—consumes me whole, salty and painful.

One could Monday-morning quarterback this thing 'til they're out of words and ready for sleep. Could bark at me like a rabid dog for not doing something, anything. Berate me for what a child I'm being. Go ahead, Dad, do it. Let me have it. Or they could justify and rationalize like Lee's doing, saying shit like "Everything's gonna be cool," and "We're in the clear," and "They were in the wrong place at the wrong time." But what everyone would fail to understand — what I can't overlook — is the guy next to me is armed and unstable, and I was just enjoying a harmless night-ride. Only a passenger.

Fuck that. Now I'm along for the ride for real.

Could all of this been prevented if I'd brought my cell phone along? Is this really *that* simple? I know I would have dialed 911 right away, would have reported the location of the accident, which might have given Lee pause; might have kept the gun in his pants. Or maybe I'd be lying dead in the field next to the young girl from California.

California.

The last thing I remember seeing as Lee pushed me into the car were the plates of the overturned coupe.

California.

And I can't stop thinking, Jason and his girl came a long way just to die.

So here we are, Lee and I, sitting on my Salvation Army couch with more money than I've ever seen spread wide on my milk crate coffee table. Stacks and stacks of rubber-banded cash. One hundred dollar bills. Benjamin Franklin's eyes spear accusations: *I discovered electricity, was a founding father of this nation. I deserve better, Jack.*

Lee slaps me hard across the face, and I finally look at him. Really look at him. He's not afraid. Nor ashamed. He's amped on adrenaline, brights at full blast, grinning like a Cheshire cat.

"Earth to Jack," he says. "You in there, man?"

No, I think. "Yes," I say.

"There's more than a hundred grand here and half is yours. Do you know what that means?"

I shake my head.

"No, you *don't* know what that means?" he says.

"No," I manage, "I don't want any part of this."

"C'mon, Ja—"

"No," I shout, the little fighter inside finally coming alive. "I want you to take all this money and leave. I don't want to see you again. Ever." The seal is broken. I'm angry now. Furious. Seeing red. Fuck you, Buddha.

Lee eases back into my couch and spreads his hands wide, a look of righteous indignation across his face. "You have to be kidding, amigo. A few hours ago I was paying your rent."

"Make your point fast then go!"

He leans forward, clutches my shoulder. "You're broke. That's my fucking point."

I wilt under the strength of his grip. Lee's a good four inches shorter than me, virtually a midget at five-four, but he's strong—spent the last few years working out, making up for what a pussy he was back in high school. I've seen him send guys much bigger than me to the hospital, and I have no doubt—even if he weren't armed—that he could end me right here.

"Think of Nora," he says, stretching out her name, making sure I know that he really knows it's not Norma.

"You're like a daddy to her, aren't you? You want to take care of—"

"Leave her out of this!" I'm grappling with survival again and ready to wipe this shit-stain off the face of the Earth. I pull away from his grip and stand. "Four months ago, I woke up. If I take this money, I'll be asleep again forever. I need you to understand two things: one, I'm not going to say shit to anyone—"

"Why would you even say that?" Lee interrupts, lifting his shirt to show me his gun. "Why would you even *think* that?"

"Fuck you, Lee. Put your fucking shirt down and listen to me. You were thinking it and so was I, so stop trying to act like a character from a Tarantino film and sober up. Number two, I want to go on with my life like this never happened, and I need you to let that happen."

Lee laughs, his face going red. "Your life," he says, "is shit."

I nod.

"Admit that," he says.

"Yeah, my life is shit."

"Say it like you mean it!"

"My life is shit," I shout. "But that's not what this is about and you know it. Now I need you to tell me we're cool, then I need you to take your shit, walk out the door, and head straight for Chicago or wherever it is you came from. Consider my half of the money repayment with interest for what you did earlier. Whatever you have to do to—"

"Are you kidding me?" Lee says, standing. "How long have we been friends, Jack?"

"Too long."

Lee lowers his head for a moment, then looks up, doing his best impersonation of someone stricken by sadness. "Come on, Jack. This isn't how I want this to go."

"You killed that girl in cold blood, Lee. You took her life for a little bit of cash."

Jack's faux-sad expression fades. "Bitch and her man almost killed us out there. You saw that, didn't you?"

"Is that how you're justifying this?"

"No. You didn't see it. You were running away like a scared little girl, weren't you?"

"Just go!"

"Jack, every sad life meets with opportunity once. This is your moment. Why can't you see that?" He gestures to the money. "This is *our* moment, man. You can open a business. I can finally settle down somewhere, stop hustling, stop running."

"What are you running from?" I snap.

"Lots of things, man, like you didn't know that already. Hell, you knew that the moment you stepped in the car with me. You know it every time I walk into your life, so don't jerk me around. Not now. Not ever again. I see the way you look at me, look down on me. I have the threads, the car, the money, and still you look down on *me*."

"That's in your head, Lee."

"You calling me crazy?"

Balling my fists, breathing so heavily I'm nearly hyperventilating, I glare at him.

"Settle down, amigo," he whispers with a smile. "C'mon, deep breaths."

"Leave," I growl.

"Look, this is meant to be, to happen just like this, this moment. How can you call something like this random?"

"I'm not. I don't think there was anything random about you killing that girl."

"Keep your voice down, okay? Just have a drink, settle down, think this through. Nora doesn't need to know where Uncle Jack got his money. She'll be in a nice school, in a better place — a room filled with stuffed animals."

I shake my head.

"Close your eyes and picture it," he says.

"No."

"You can help Lily, too," he says. "You can clean her up, take her away from here, away from her demons."

"Get out, Lee. Out of town. Out of my life. I don't fuck with you; you don't fuck with me."

"And you're okay with that? All of the guilt, none of the reward?"

"I didn't kill anyone."

Lee lowers his head and grins, his intense glare still slicing me to shreds. "You know what I mean, Jack. I know how you are, how things...eat you up inside. I grew up with you, don't you remember? I probably know you better than you know me; better than you know yourself."

"I woke up."

Lee starts putting the money back in the Hello Kitty bag. "Woke up, huh?" Then he slings the pack over his shoulder and sticks out his right hand. Tentatively, I take his hand to shake. He grips tightly, pulls me close. I can feel his gun against my crotch.

"No bullshit," he growls in my ear. "No changing your mind."

I shake my head, and he pulls me closer. Tighter. I can hardly breathe.

"I love you," he says. "That's the only reason I'm letting you live. I fucking love you, man."

He lets go, and I gasp for air.

Finally, the door slams, and he's gone.

Big cities have their 7-Elevens and Quick Trips, but we have the Millie-Mart. Don't ask about the name, 'cause I already have and no one understands it. The place stays open 'til midnight, less than fifteen minutes from now, and that's a small blessing. My head is pounding, and I need a cigarette bad.

"Camel blues," I say.

Fluorescents five minutes from death flicker. The girl behind the counter—her name is Rita, and I went to high school with her—looks away from her phone and shoots me a funny look. "Didn't you quit smoking for your niece?" she asks.

Everyone knows everyone's business 'round here. Except the dark stuff. That shit we stow deep.

"Guess I'm not that strong after all," I manage.

She laughs, but she can tell I'm struggling with something more than a mere addiction to nicotine. "Quitting's easy," she says, "I've done it hundreds of times." If this were a text message, here's where the "LOL" would go. She's got it written on her forehead.

Loser Zero Loser.

That thought normally brings a smile to my face. Am I smiling now? Maybe. I don't know. I can't even feel my face.

I pay for the cigarettes, grab an American-flag matchbook from the counter, and step outside.

The first drag hits my palate like ass, the way a cigarette really tastes before we immunize our senses to them. Trudging homeward, I take long drags, and still my head throbs.

The night is still; the moon, now high, shrouded in clouds and no longer bleeding. It feels like rain. That's good. We need rain—a strong, long storm to wash away the grime.

Outside my apartment, beside a tree, the Labrador I fed earlier is curled in a ball.

"Hey," I say, clapping my hands. "Hey, boy, get up." The dog could be a girl, of course; not like I've checked the sex or cared to notice, but still I clap and repeat, "Hey, boy."

The mutt doesn't stir, and that's when the tears start gushing.

The girl from California is dead.

The black dog is dead.

And I sense that I'm not too far behind them. These things, they always come in threes.

WEDNESDAY

CHAPTER FIVE

Finding your place in the world boils down to one thing: The struggle for identity. All of us: in search of our talents, our purpose, trying to make sense of our time and place on this big blue ball. In my twenty-seven years, I've only been good at one thing.

Being Uncle Jack.

This is where I train my brain as I lie in the haze between sleep and waking. The sun slices through the blinds, smudging focus. All I can see is light. And I know, I know, I know that I have to disengage from last night. What I witnessed…that shit never happened. Only a nightmare.

"A nightmare," I repeat in a whisper.

There's a knock at the door.

A nightmare.

Another knock sounds, this time louder, and I'm terrified that terror still reigns. I slide off my futon, pull on a T-shit, and the knocking, it continues. As I trudge for the door, I convince myself of something: If it's Lee, I'm in. No turning back, I'll take the money. But if it's anyone else, anyone at all, the nightmare's dead.

Dead.

A voice calls through the door: "Come on, Jack, open up. I know you're in there." It's Lily, and I breathe a sigh of relief.

"Let me put on some pants," I call out, scratching my ass. "I just woke up."

I snatch a pair of jeans from the floor by the couch, slide them on, then open the door. Standing there are my sister and niece. Nora's smiling, always smiling, and that makes me smile. Lily, however, doesn't look so hot. She's gaunt from all the meth, shaking, holding onto Nora's hand like it's salvation. My sister, she loves her daughter. I know this. Problem is, she doesn't love herself. Never has. Hate to get all Oprah about the whole thing, but that bitch, she works in oceans of truth. She and Buddha would make quite a couple.

"Jesus, Jack," Lily says, "I've been trying to call you all morning. It's three in the afternoon."

"Rough night," I say, still smiling at Nora. I wink, then turn to Lily and ask, "What's up?"

"I have some things I need to do," she replies. "When do you work next?"

"Saturday. You know that, Lil. Always the same schedule—Tuesday and Saturday."

"Can I leave Nora with you?"

"Sure," I say, now smiling at my niece again. "For how long?"

"No more than a day," Lily says. Nora breaks away from her mother, gallops into the apartment, wraps me in a hug. I lift her, hold her close.

"I missed you, Uncle Jack," she says.

"Missed you, too," I reply.

Then she pulls her head back and glares at me. "You stink like smokes."

I put her down, shrug, and say, "Had some friends over last night."

Lily's stare becomes accusatory. "Yeah," she says, "I've seen Lee driving around town. Rough night, huh?"

"Rough night," I agree.

"That car of his," Lily says, "it's just his way of making up for a small dick."

I shoot her a *leave-it-alone* look, but she's already turning to leave. She stops, looks back, and manages a weak, crooked smile. "Thanks, Jack," she says.

I nod as I close the door.

The nightmare's over.

Here I am with Nora. She's jumping up and down on the couch as I take our food from the DQ bag and set it on the old card table by the kitchenette.

"I heard some new jokes," she says. "You wanna hear 'em?"

I eat a French fry, take a drink of badly mixed Sprite, then say, "Yeah, 'course I do."

She jumps off the couch, runs to the table, and plops into the plastic deck chair I've set out for her. I have three deck chairs but no deck.

"Man oh man," she says, "I'm starved," then takes a big bite of burger.

"Well," I say. "What about those jokes?"

She giggles, takes another bite, then, mouth full, says, "I like your jokes better, Uncle Jack. You tell me one. A funny one...*please.*"

"When have my jokes ever *not* been funny?"

She giggles again. "Dunno," she says. "Just make it good this time."

The spotlight's always on me when I'm with her, but I don't mind. I sit down at the rickety table and scratch my chin. "Let me think," I say. "Hmmm...funny jokes, eh?"

"Come on, Uncle Jack."

I'm searching my mind for age-appropriate humor, coming up empty. She enjoys this part of the show, the part where I struggle. She once brought over a Casio keyboard and watched me as I made up stupid songs for hours, hitting random keys. Never had a lesson and it showed, but she loved every minute nonetheless. Her favorite was a little ditty set to the keyboard's slowest Salsa beat. I called it "Slow Jam."

Slow Jam,

Toe Jam,

No Ma'am (repeat).

I haven't mentioned this yet, but I'm a fucking poet.

Finally, a dumb joke pops into my head, and I say, "Why do bees hum?"

"How would I know?" Her reaction, of course, is a hell of a lot funnier than the punch line could ever hope to be. Here I am, repeating some shit I likely read on a candy package as a kid, but Nora's entranced. An important thing I've learned about kids: The act of telling, the effort, is always more important than the actual words; long as the words are always kind.

"Bees don't know the words to the song," I say, spreading my hands wide and waiting for the laugh. "Huh? Pretty funny, right?"

Nora squints and says, "I thought you were gonna tell a *funny* one."

"Hey," I say, unwrapping my chicken sandwich, "if I'd known you were coming over I'd have written some new material."

That's clearly funny, 'cause now she laughs. Then she says, "I've got one."

"Hit me."

"Okay, let me see if I can get this right. I don't know if I know what this means or not, so you got to tell me if it's funny, okay?"

"Don't go blue on me, Bear." That's my name for her. *Bear.* Don't know where I got it or what it means, but she likes it and that's all that matters.

"Huh?"

"Just tell your joke."

"Okay. Let's see. There was a mommy and a daddy, and the daddy loved the mommy very, very much. So...um...he decided that he wanted to show the mommy how much he loved her, and so he traveled all over the place. He climbed the highest mountains and he swimmed the deepest oceans. He went to the most enchanting places in the whole wide world, and everywhere he went, he bought the mommy a special present, so she would know that he loved her more than anything in the whole wide world." Eyes wide, she takes a deep breath. I love it when she gets into telling a story. I keep telling her she should be a writer someday. "One day," she continues, "he finally came home, excited to show her everything he'd got for her, to tell her about all of his adventures. Do you know what the mommy said?"

"Thank you," I say, throwing a wadded wrapper at the trashcan and missing. "So much for that NBA contract."

Nora shakes her head. "Are you listening?"

"Of course, go on."

"Okay," she says. "Now, you have to tell me if this is funny, okay?"

"I will."

"Promise, 'cause I really don't get it. I mean, I get it, but I don't get why it's a joke."

"Yeah, Bear, I promise."

"The mommy doesn't say anything."

Now it's my turn to squint. "Why doesn't she say anything?"

"She doesn't say anything 'cause she took their kids and left him 'cause he was never ever home."

There are no words for that incredibly sad punch line, and I just sit there.

"So," she says, "is it funny?"

"Where did you hear that?" I ask.

"Samantha Bradley told it to me at school. It just kinda stuck in my earballs."

Earballs—I taught her that one, a funny-sounding make-believe word that's out of synch with the throat-slitting riddle she's just dealt. I shake my head slowly. "No," I say, "it's not funny. Not funny at all."

"That's what I thought, too."

"Are Samantha's parents divorced?"

Nora looks confused by this question. "Dunno. What's that got to do with a joke?"

There's a moment of silence while she finishes her dinner. When done, she looks up at me, a little blotch of ketchup on her cheek, and says, "What are we doing next?"

I'm still thinking about that morose joke—hardly a joke—trying to figure out why it would stick in a kid's head. I reach a napkin to her face and wipe the ketchup away. Profanity I could understand, even accept, particularly given her mother's ways, but I just wasn't ready for the *Ordinary People* edition of children's humor.

"Uncle Jack," she says, "you okay?"

I snap out of it. "Yeah, yeah. Hey, do you know what I forgot at Dairy Queen?"

"No, what?"

"Ice cream. You wanna go for a walk and get some?"

She jumps up and shouts, "Yay!"

CHAPTER SIX

We take a lot of walks, Nora and I. Normally she skips
around me and asks questions. Always with the questions.
As we walk now, however, through the unseasonably cool
evening (the flatlands occasionally get a break from
extremes), she's silent, holding my hand tightly. I like this,
makes me feel she needs me.

Halfway to our destination, I ask, "What's wrong,
Bear?"

She looks up and says, "Nothing's wrong with *me*,
Uncle Jack."

And I realize the tables have turned. The need is mine.
I never would have believed a child could operate on such
an advanced frequency, but—trust me—Nora gets more
about the human condition than most twice her age, even
if she's emotionally stunted in some ways, for which I
credit her mother.

"What?" I say. "You think there's something wrong
with me?"

She grips my hand a little tighter and starts swinging
it. Nothing is said between us for a while. Then, right as
we're stepping up to the window of the DQ, and a hell of a

lot louder than I'd like, she asks, "Why are you single, Uncle Jack?"

The cute girl behind the order window clearly hears this. "Why are you single, Uncle Jack?" the DQ girl repeats with a giggle. I've never seen her before. She's wiping the counter, her smile now trained on Nora, who's returning it in a conspiratorial manner. There's nothing premeditated or dark about the cunning ways of my niece, but let me just say, she is an opportunistic and lovely manipulator. Forget Buddha. Nora would make a wonderful used car salesman.

To Nora, I nervously ask, "What would you like?"

"Hot fudge sundae," she chirps. "Same as always."

"Two hot fudge sundaes," I say as I slide a ten dollar bill across the counter.

"What sizes?" the girl asks, still smiling. Big blue eyes. Long red hair. Pale skin, which I like even though it's out of fashion at the moment. Very cute and quaint in her blue and red company tee. The mole on her neck is peeking through layers of concealer, as are her freckles, but she should let her blemishes breathe. Here's the thing most women don't understand about men, at least the kind of men who aren't douchebags: most of us love imperfections. Yeah, we're a kinky bunch.

"Small," I say. I'm trying to act cool, but I can feel my lips quivering and my hands shaking. It's pretty rare to run into someone I don't know, and I can't seem to internalize my discomfort. Par for the course, I guess, when you spend your entire life in a place that makes Mayberry look urban.

The girl takes the money and turns to make the sundaes, and I kneel down to Nora. "What are you doing?" I whisper.

"Thought you could use a girlfriend is all," she says, then holds a hand to her mouth, trying not to bust out laughing.

I hook a thumb toward the order window. "Do you know this girl?"

"No," Nora says, a little bit of laughter escaping around her hand. "That's why I did it."

"And you think it's that easy?"

"Happens all the time, doesn't it?"

There's really no arguing with her on the count. Like it or not, every loser has to realize this simple truth eventually.

I stand and discover the girl is already at the window with our ice cream, my change sitting on the counter. Her kind eyes tell me she's been standing there a little longer than I'd like, listening to the conversation.

I put a buck in the tip jar, the rest of the change in my pocket, and hand my niece her sundae. "Hey, Nora," I say, "why don't you have a seat, okay? I'll be right along."

"Yessir," Nora says with a comical salute, then saunters toward one of the patio tables, eating as she goes.

"She's adorable," says the girl.

"My niece," I say.

"Yeah, I gathered that from 'Uncle Jack.'"

"Are you new around here?"

She nods. "Moved here this week."

"Can I ask why?"

"You can ask, but I'd be more likely to answer over dinner."

"What's your name?"

"Paige." She sticks her hand out the window. "And it's nice to meet you, Uncle Jack."

I take her hand, powerful but feminine, and we shake. "Nice to meet you, too, but please...don't call me Uncle Jack."

She laughs.

"When?" I ask.

"When what, Jack?"

God, I love the way my name sounds on her tongue. "When do you want to go to dinner?"

"Saturday," she says. "That's my first day off."

"Is today your first day on?"

"Bingo."

"And you're working the place alone? No training? Hell, I was here less than an hour ago and —"

"It's the DQ," she says with a laugh. "I'm not launching the space shuttle for NASA."

"Well, yeah, but —"

"And this isn't my first ice cream shack."

"Is it your last?"

"God, I hope so."

We both laugh.

"I gotta get this out of the way," I say. "I don't have a car."

"Neither do I, Jack. I'll just meet you in front of this place at six. We'll go from there, okay?"

"Can we make it six-thirty? I usually get off work after five, and I'd like to take a shower before we go out?"

"Mighty long shower."

"What can I say? — I like to be clean."

"I won't even touch that one."

"You okay with coffee shop food?"

"What other choice do we have?"

I shake my head and smile, confidence rising. I look back at Nora. She's halfway through her ice cream and grinning at us.

"See you Saturday?" I say.

"Not if I see you first."

"How did you get so smart, Bear?" I ask, sitting down at the rusty patio table. She's already made history of her dessert, and I've yet to start into mine, which is melting down the plastic container and making my hand sticky.

"I do go to school," she says, "when it's not summer out."

I shrug then start eating.

"Momma says you're sad," Nora blurts. "She thinks it's because you're all alone."

I consider this for a moment, take another bite, then ask, "What do you think?"

"Sometimes, but not always. I think Momma's really the sad one."

"Why do you say that?"

"Dunno. Just is, I guess. Can't really 'splain it. She's got her boyfriend, Craig, but I've never met him."

"You're not missing much," I say, even though I shouldn't.

Nora remains bright. Never darkens, that one. "Yeah, that's what Momma says, too."

"Does she cry a lot?"

"Who?"

"Your mom, silly."

"No. Should she?"

"Isn't that what sad people do?"

"Sure, in movies or if they're *crazy*." She wiggles her hands and shakes her body as she says *crazy*. Then she adds, "The only time I cry is when I get hurt. Like when I fell off the swing set and cut my lip." She's peeling back her lower lip to show me the scar, which, as far as I can tell, isn't really there anymore.

"You'll learn," I say.

"Learn what?"

"To cry."

"Why would I want to learn that?"

"No one escapes. Sorry."

"Sounds pretty lame."

"Yeah, it's lame."

"You seemed sad earlier, but you look much better now."

I chuckle. "All thanks to you."

She returns the laugh, then says, "Am I weird?"

"What makes you ask that?"

"'Cause I don't get sad like you and Momma?"

"No. Not at all. I'd say that makes you lucky."

After that long volley, Nora has a lot to think about, and I take this time to relax.

A nice evening, cool and peaceful. Birds sing and crickets chirp. These moments are rare, and I lean back and breathe this one in. Nora does the same, apparently as content with the notion of being "lucky" as I am with the possibility of getting lucky on Saturday.

Damn, I haven't been on a date in more than a year, but I'm trying not to get my hopes up. And that's not tough, 'cause here, in this moment of quiet, I realize... No, I know. I'm running low on hope and far from all right.

Here we are, thousands of miles away from firefights in the Middle East; far removed from any kind of real hardship that isn't self-inflicted. Ours are, in many ways, the problems of paradise. Yet...

I pray to a god I still don't believe in, trying to push away the memory of last night; pray that Lee's driving to Chicago right now. I'm afraid his black Mustang will glide down Main Street. That he'll stop in for a banana split and ruin my calm. But that's not happening, and the notion is a million miles from any concern Nora has. So I let myself just be—what else can I do?—taking deep breaths and repeating *everything's gonna be all right* in my head. Because everything has to be. Has to get better. Darkness can't possibly last forever, can it?

I close my eyes and hear the engine of a sports car.

"What's wrong, Uncle Jack?"

I'm just hearing things. It will go away.

"Nothing," I say, but I feel my smile cracking. "Everything's fine."

The race of the approaching engine grows unmistakably real, and I feel my body shifting gears. Peace ebbing. Tension mounting.

Shhhuck, shhhuck, shhhuck.

"You don't look fine," she says.

"I am," I insist. "I am."

Shhuck, shhhuck, shhhuck.

When I open my eyes, Lee's pulling into the parking lot, a big grin splitting his mug.

And Nora's right. I'm five thousand miles from fine.

CHAPTER SEVEN

Lee, of course, doesn't head to the window and order a banana split. He walks right over and sits in the chair between me and Nora. She isn't saying anything, but I can tell she's uncomfortable. Stranger danger warnings seem to be going off in her head, but I'm with her, and that's where her gaze lies. Girl knows how to find her anchor in a storm.

"*Nora*," he says, drawing out her name as if to tell me he really knows it and always has.

"Who are you?" she asks.

Lee looks over at me, mouth agape. "You mean to tell me that your Uncle Jack here hasn't told you about me, his best friend? I'm your Uncle Lee?"

"My momma talks about you sometimes," Nora says, "but not Uncle Jack."

"What do you want, Lee?" I ask. "Can't you see I'm watching my niece right now?"

"Hey," Lee says, "I love kids." He rustles Nora's hair, and the gesture causes her to look irritated as she backs away from his hand. At eleven, she's a far better judge of character than I am at twenty-seven. Then again, my cat hated Lee, too, so what does that say about me?

"What do you want, Lee?" I repeat, raising my brow and trying to keep the anger out of my voice for Nora's sake.

"Cool down, amigo," Lee says, waving defensive hands. "Was just driving by and saw you. Thought I'd swing in and say hi, maybe spread the good word of the Lord."

"I don't believe in God," I say.

Lee feigns surprise and covers his ears. "Not in front of the *child*."

"I don't believe in God, either," Nora says.

"See," says Lee. "See what you're doing. You're corrupting a child, taking away her salvation."

Standing, I reach around the other side of the table and take Nora's hand. As we start away from Lee, he says, "God brought us together last night, Jack."

"Come on, Nora," I say. "Keep walking. Ignore him."

"You can't deny it," Lee calls out. "It was God that brought us and Jason and Jenny together last night."

Jenny?

I turn to Paige, who's staring at me through the order window. "Sounds like you've got some trouble," she says.

"Yeah," I say, keeping my voice low. "Psycho friend from high school. Nothing serious. Look, can you keep an eye on Nora for a minute while I talk to this guy?"

"Sure," Paige says. She swings the door next to the order window open. "Come on in, sweetheart."

Nora pensively walks toward Paige as I turn to Lee.

He's sitting there, glib as he ever was, just waiting for me to walk back to him. To admit that I need the money, that I need him. So I take a deep breath, march up to him, and growl, "Stay the fuck away from me."

Lee shakes his head. "That's no way to talk to your savior."

"What do I have to do, Lee? What?"

"Just take your half of the money. It's in the car. I can give it to you now."

"No. I don't want any part of that, and I don't want anything to do with you." I pull out my cell phone and hold it up. "Take off right now, Lee, or I'm going to dial 911 and report what happened last night."

"Then who will take care of Nora, Jack? 'Cause trust me, you're gonna go away for a while, too. I'll make sure of that. I'll make sure I tell the cops it was your idea."

"They won't buy that."

"Maybe not, but you sure did take your time reporting it. At this point, you're an accomplice whether you dirty your hands with the loot or not."

"So you're an expert on the law now?"

Lee laughs. "Break enough of 'em and, yeah, you learn a thing or two."

I heave a sigh and look back at the DQ. Paige is showing Nora how the ice cream machines work, but Nora isn't paying attention. She's looking at me, and there's something new in her eyes. *Fear.* I've never seen it there before, and I'll do anything to make it go away.

I turn to Lee. "And that's it?"

"That's it," he says.

"I take it and we're done?"

"Take it and Tuesday's gone with the wind."

"Okay."

Lee gets up and starts for his car. I turn to Nora and call, "I'll be back in a second."

Lee already has the trunk open when I get to the Mustang. "I got you a little present," he says, then hands me a briefcase. "Samsonite. Very durable."

"Gee, thanks."

"Don't mention it. My grandpa used to sell the damn things, and Gram still has a bunch of 'em in her junk closet. Thought you might like this better than a Hello Kitty backpack."

I take the case, much lighter on my hand than my soul. "So that's it?" I ask.

"You know, it hurts that you're so anxious to get rid of me."

I groan. "Look, Lee, you can't really — "

"I know, amigo, but you could at least wish me luck."

"Good luck," I say.

With that, Lee wraps me in a bear hug. "Maybe," he says, his voice sincere for the first time in recent memory, "just maybe we can put this behind us some day, huh?"

"Yeah," I say. "Maybe."

"Good enough," he says. "I love you, man."

"Hey, Lee. Who's Jenny? Where did that name come from?"

He laughs darkly, looks away for a moment, then his eyes snap back to mine. Locked and loaded. "Bitch left her ID in the bag. Jennifer Snowdon of Sacramento."

"Sacramento? What the hell were they doing in the middle of nowhere?"

Lee laughs again. "What are any of us doing here, my man?"

"Take care, Lee. Be careful, okay?"

"Always."

I start toward the DQ as Lee revs the Mustang's engine. He peels out, leaving a cloud of dust in his wake, but I'm moving slow, feeling tired and defeated. Nora rushes for me, puts her arms around me. "What was that?" she whispers.

"Not now," I say.

"Everything okay?" Paige asks.

"Yeah," I say. "Thanks for keeping an eye on Nora."

"No problem," she says. "I like kids."

"Look, about Saturday…"

"You're not going to break our date are you?"

"Well, I wanted to give you a chance to."

"Why?"

"I've got to be honest, Paige, I'm a mess."

"Come here," she says, leaning over the counter.

I approach, swallowing the dry lump in my throat, trying not to cry.

She moves close to me, and I can smell her shampoo, something with apples, and her perfume, something cheap but wildly intoxicating. In a near-whisper, she says, "I'm working at a Dairy Queen in God's ass crack, not the executive suite of Bank of America, mister. So, if it's all right with you, I'm a fucking mess, too."

I chuckle, and she gives me a quick kiss on the cheek.

"See you on Saturday," she says.

"Saturday," I agree, and things seem almost bearable again.

CHAPTER EIGHT

When we get back to my apartment, having said nothing on the walk home, Nora turns on the TV and starts rummaging through the DVDs she keeps at my place. It's getting dark now, and she's winding down, but she likes to watch cartoons before bed. Classic Hanna Barbara — *Yogi Bear, The Flintstones*; her favorite is *Yakky Doodle*, and that's the disc she pops into the player.

"Hey, Bear," I say.

"Yeah."

"I'll be right back, 'kay?"

As I start for my room, Nora says, "Uncle Jack?"

"What is it, hon?"

"What's in that thing your friend gave you?"

There it is, the million dollar question I dreaded all the way home. "Nothing to worry about," I say. "Just watch your toons and I'll be right back."

"Okay, Uncle Jack," she says in a squeaky voice, doing a passable impersonation of Yakky.

I smile for her benefit, then, in a gentle but strained voice, say, "Keep the volume down, all right? Don't wanna get in deep with our neighbors again."

I walk into the bedroom as duck-call music starts playing, close the door, and toss the briefcase on my unmade futon. Then I reach below the makeshift bed and pull out the cigar box where I store my savings. I flip the cigar box open, then spring the latches on the old Samsonite.

Two amounts of money glare back at me—large versus paltry; wrong versus right.

A wave of emotion hits me like a hammer, and everything I've been denying, bottling up, justifying... Every goddamn thing knocks me down all at once, illusions and delusions disintegrating in a flash.

Fresh out of excuses, I kneel in front of my futon and weep.

Covered in sweat, I wake with a gasp. Someone's knocking at my door, and all I can think about is Nora. My heart's pounding, racing faster than my nervous system can process. And it's dark. Too dark.

A shadow—diminutive and familiar, thank God— moves into the open doorway. "Uncle Jack," Nora says. "Who's here?"

"I don't know," I say. "Get in my room and don't come out 'til I tell you to." I hate myself for sounding hysterical, but I can't help it. I flip on the light and snatch the Louisville Slugger I keep propped against the wall, then I close the bedroom.

The knocking intensifies as I creep toward the front door. Finally, I shout, "Who's there?"

"It's me," replies the exasperated, breathless voice of my sister.

I drop the bat and open the door. She looks worse than I've ever seen her. Even a few feet away, I can smell booze, lots of it, and she's swaying back and forth, eyelids fluttering.

"Lily," I say, reaching out to her.

"You're not her dad," she shouts.

"Keep it down and come inside."

"I'm here to get my daughter, bring her home where she belongs."

I can already hear neighbors waking up through the paper-thin walls of the multi-plex. Nerves shot, I plead, "Keep it down, Lil. Come inside and I'll make some coffee."

"I don't want your fucking coffee, and I don't want your fucking charity. You're my little brother, and I'm s'posed to take care of you, not the other way 'round."

"Come on, Lily. Come inside and we'll talk."

"Where's Nora? Where's my baby? I wanna take my baby and go, get as far away from this place as I can."

"It's late, Lil. She needs sleep. Come in. Stay the night. You can take her home in the morning, when you're sober."

"I'll take her whenever I damn well please. She's my daughter. Not yours. You're my brother—my *baby* brother."

"Momma," Nora says, stepping into the living room.

"Baby," Lily chokes, kneeling down and holding out her arms. "You wanna come home with Momma, don't you?"

Nora shakes her head and moves behind me for protection. "What's wrong with her?" Lily demands.

I'll say this for Lily: she's done a fair job of shielding her daughter from the monster she's capable of being. She picked a fine time to drop the mask.

Lily glares at me, still on her knees, looking like some kind of hunched-over witch in an old horror film or a Shakespeare revival. "You're turning my girl against me, aren't you?" she wheezes.

"Lily," I plead, "stay the night and we can talk in the morning. You're in no shape to—"

"Fuck you," she says, then lunges at me, scratching and clawing.

Nora screams and runs into the bedroom.

"I'm calling the police," Sam Winslow, the guy who lives next door, shouts from outside.

"Stop it," I scream, but Lily keeps coming, hammering me. I wrap her tightly in my arms, carry her outside, and slam the front door.

"Give me my daughter," she cries through cheap wood.

"The police will be here any minute," I say. "Do you want them to search you for drugs? Do you want to go away for a while?"

Silence.

"Come back tomorrow," I say.

But she's already gone. I can hear her car peeling away and Nora crying in my room.

As I explain everything to two county cops, all I can think about is the money in the other room. Can they see it on my face? Are they making mental notes to get a search warrant? Still, I manage to articulate the situation, and they nod and express something approaching genuine concern.

"You have any idea where your sister went?"

"Either home or back to her boyfriend's," I answer.

"Boyfriend's name?"

"Craig Strickland."

"Sorry to hear that."

"Yeah," I say, "sorry to say it."

This goes on for another few minutes, until the cops thank me for my time, remind me to keep the volume down (clearly for the benefit of the eavesdropping neighbors), then leave.

Nora's curled up on the couch, shell-shocked. I've never seen her like this. I sit on the edge of the couch and grab her foot. "Bear," I say.

She unwraps herself from her blankets and looks at me, and I can see she's crying.

I take her in my arms and whisper assurances. "Everything's going to be all right." But why should she believe me if I don't even believe myself?

"I'm learning," she mutters into my ear.

I tighten my embrace and say, "That's okay," wishing she didn't have to grow up so soon.

THURSDAY

CHAPTER NINE

We slog through our morning, eating cereal, watching television, hardly saying a word. Summer's back in full swing, my AC-free apartment sweltering. Fans rattle and hum in the living room and bedroom windows, but little good they do.

My head throbs, and I think about going into the bathroom to smoke one of my few remaining cigarettes. No. I don't want to leave Nora alone. Her condition is critical in my estimation, and I need to stay with her, careful not to push. When she's ready to talk, I'm ready to listen.

A former boy band member is showing the audience of some talk show how to make authentic linguini when my cell phone chirps. I pull it out of my pocket. The incoming call is from an unknown number. The time is 10:21 a.m. I almost let the call roll to voicemail, but curiosity gets the best of me.

"Hello," I say.

"Is this Jack Lewis?" a commanding female voice asks.

"Yeah, this is Jack."

"Mr. Lewis," she says, "This is Dr. Phyllis Marshall from Memorial Hospital in Seward. Your sister, Ms. Lily Lewis, has you listed as her emergency contact. Do I have the correct person?"

"Yes." I say, barely breathing.

"Let me assure you, Mr. Lewis, that your sister is under my care. That said, she was injured early this morning and was rushed to our facility."

"Is she going to be okay?"

This gets Nora's attention. Eyes wide, she approaches

"I can't comment on that, Mr. Lewis, hospital policy, but I will tell you that we've made the decision not to admit her to an ICU in Lincoln. That should give you some indication of her prognosis. Are there any other family members you'd like us to contact, or will you be able to handle things on your end?"

"I think I've got it covered," I say. "If I may ask, what happened?"

"Mr. Lewis, I wish I could tell you more, but I think it's best if your sister explains the rest to you and your family."

"Yes, of course. Thank you."

"Good day, Mr. Lewis."

Nora's in my face. "Momma?" she asks. "What's wrong with Momma?"

I drop the phone onto the couch and bury my face in my palms.

"What is it, Uncle Jack?"

"Your mom's in the hospital, Bear."

"Is she okay?"

"She's hurt, but she's going to be fine."

"Are we going to visit her?"

"She's in Seward."

"That's way too far to walk."

"I know."

"So how are we going to get there?"

I know the right answer, but I don't like it.

"We have to go, Uncle Jack. We have to."

"I know. Don't worry."

"But how are we going to get there?" Her voice is frantic now, and I'm not used to hearing her like this. I don't like it, but I have to put my internal bullshit calculator away and cut to the quick.

"We're going to see your grandpa," I say.

Amidst a scorched-earth sea of yellow and brown lies an anomaly—my father's lawn, a lush patch of green that stands out like a landing strip for aliens. In-ground sprinklers sputter and rosebushes beam with halos of honeybees as Nora and I walk to the front door, a crimson, opulent-looking thing that's out of place on the ranch-style tract house circa 1964. The house where I grew up. The house I haven't been in for more than a decade.

"Wow," Nora says. "Fancy."

The big red N above the door screams "No," though I know it only speaks to Dad's eternal love for college football. God, I hate how crazy this state goes for their beloved Huskers, but it could be worse—I could live in Texas.

Nora smiles as the doorbell chimes jingle and jangle some long-forgotten tune.

Then the door opens, and here he is. Chuck Lewis. Dad. More gray in his hair and beard than I remember, but otherwise, same as he ever was. His face is washed with momentary confusion, or is it surprise? Both, probably. Slowly, a smile takes shape then dissolves. "What's wrong?" he says.

"This is your granddaughter," I say, "Nora."

"Nora," he repeats slowly, looking down at her. Smiling for real, he extends a hand. "It's nice to meet you, Nora."

"Momma's hurt. She's in the hospital."

Shaking Nora's hand, he casts terrified eyes my way. "Lily?"

I nod. "We need to get to her, Chuck. Thought you could drive us, and…"

"And what, son?" he asks.

"And we thought you should know."

"I appreciate that. Is she…is Lily all right?"

I shrug. "She'll live, if that's what you're asking, but…I don't know."

Still gripping the old man's hand, thankfully changing the tone of this awkward exchange, Nora says, "It's nice to meet you, too…Grandpa?"

He turns back to her, trying to put his best salesman smile back in place. "That's right, sweetie. I'm your grandpa." He lets go of her, then adds, "So…how 'bout a hug instead of a handshake?"

"But we already shook?"

"Just like your mom when she was wee," he says with a laugh. "Well then, Professor, how 'bout a handshake *and* a hug?"

They embrace as I push back tears. Much as I hate to admit it, since it's largely my fault, this is off beam — Nora just now meeting Chuck, and under the present circumstances.

Chuck? Dad?

I can't reconcile the name with the man's biological stance. Best to stick with Chuck. For now.

"Come inside," he says, moving into profile and motioning into the house.

The cool air hits me, then I see Henrietta atop a tall bookshelf, wide eyes looking down at me. But it can't be her, my beloved cat. She'd have to be —

The cat leaps onto a couch, then the floor, and ambles to me.

"Henrietta hardly moves for anyone anymore," Chuck says. "But she clearly remembers you, son."

"How old is she?" I ask, kneeling down and running my hands through her matted fur. A little rougher for wear, but it's her. All the markings I remember: the orange M above her brow; the question mark-shaped coils that wrap around her hind legs. She purrs for me, no weaker for age, as I stroke behind her ears.

"Twenty-one," he replies. "Old enough to drink. Thought about giving her a beer to celebrate, but —" He laughs. "I want this old girl to stick around as long as she can. She's the only thing that connects me to..." He trails off sadly as Henrietta rubs her chin against my face.

"Boy oh boy," Chuck says, regaining his steam, "she sure missed you."

Nora plops on the couch and says, "When're we leaving for the hospital?"

Chuck takes her measure, a hand on his hip. "In a rush, are we, Professor?"

"Why do you call me that?" she asks.

"Professor?"

"Yeah."

"'Cause I can tell just how smart you are."

She smiles and says, "Thanks. But when are going to leave?"

Chuck laughs, and I can't help but join him. He turns to me and says, "She's exactly like Lily was, isn't she?"

I hadn't noticed, but he's right, and I nod agreement. "We are anxious to get going, Chuck?"

"Can't you call me dad?" he asks, keeping his voice low and directed at me. "It would really mean a lot."

"Will it get us into the car?" I ask.

Pain sweeps his face for a moment, then he wipes it away. "Okay, okay," he says, "but on one condition. You guys are my guests for dinner tonight." He turns to Nora. "Would you like that, Professor? Hamburgers, hotdogs, a little KC-style barbecue? I run a pretty mean grill."

Nora looks to me for approval, and I mouth *yes*, though part of me—the part I'm doing my best to kill—screams no.

She stands, curtsies like a princess in a Disney film, and says, "We'd be honored, dear sir."

And that gesture wipes any trace of pain from the old man's face.

CHAPTER TEN

Chuck and Nora are in the waiting room because I wanted — needed — this moment alone with my sister. Also, I didn't want to hit her with too much at once.

Lily looks like hell, the right side of her face bruised beyond recognition. The heart monitor beeps reassuringly, and she does her best to smile at me. A few of her teeth are missing, her lips rough with scar tissue.

"Where's Nora?" she asks in a drugged, dreamy voice.

"She's in the waiting room, Lil."

"But...but who's—"

"Chuck," I say, tears welling in my eyes.

"Was afraid of that," she mutters. "My own damn fault."

With a curt nod, I say, "He...he loves her, Lil. He's good with—"

"He destroyed us," she says. "Destroyed our family, Jack. Don't you remember?"

"I don't know. I've been thinking about that a lot lately, and—"

"It's true and you know it. We've been over this time and time again—it's not a question of—"

"We need him, Lil." I'm trying to keep my voice soft, but that's a battle I'm losing. Her stupidity has me seething, but I'm holding onto my shit for the most part, surprising myself.

"Can I see Nora?" she asks.

"In a minute," I say. "First, I want to know what the hell happened."

Her eyes dance around, avoiding me, then settle on the room's sole window. In a low, degraded wheeze, she says, "I went back to Craig's."

"And...?"

"High as a kite. He was...worse than ever. I tried reasoning with him, then tried to leave, but—"

"You weren't in a very reasonable mood yourself last night," I say.

Her eyes shoot back to me, filled with tears. "I'm sorry," she mutters. "I'll change, I promise. I'm done with him, done with self-medicating, done with feeling sorry for myself."

"Sorry, but I've heard that song already."

"I'm a fuck up, Jack, but you have to believe me this time." She's weeping now. "He hurt me so bad, Jack. I thought...I thought I was going to die...that I'd leave Nora motherless... I just need to see her. I just need to see my little girl and let her know Momma's gonna be all right."

She holds a hand out to me, and I take it. Frail. Feeble.

"Thank you," she says.

"For what?" I ask.

"For being Uncle Jack. For looking after my Nora. For being everything I haven't. And thank you...thank you for standing your ground last night. Was a time when...when you wouldn't have stood up like that."

"But it sent you back to him."

"No... That was my choice, all mine. Can you imagine if I'd gotten in a car accident last night? With Nora in the...with *my baby* in the car?"

"Don't think about that," I say. "It didn't go down that way."

"I'm a terrible mother—worse than Mom."

"Don't say that. Don't—"

"I don't want to see him, Jack."

I let go of her hand and pace around the room, then, looking through the window, I watch a robin building a nest in a nearby tree. Finally, I say, "He'll be hurt."

"Good... I hurt, too, and I'm not talking about the shit Craig did. Painkillers are taking care of that, and I've already cornered the market on everything else. No drug does the trick, Jack. Nothing makes me forget."

"I understand, but I don't think we're supposed to forget, Lil. I think we're supposed to forgive."

"Give me a little more time."

"I will."

"Good. Now...if you don't mind, I *need* to see my baby."

After I walk Nora to Lily's room, I wander the small hospital. Thing is, I'm not far removed from her in the feelings department; not ready to be alone with Chuck and have a real talk.

Lily and I, we never talk about what he did. Not with real words. We just remind each other, like Mom did for so long, that he's bad. What we do, really, is we feed each other hate. And hate, well, she's a big fat bitch who likes to be fed.

So this is me, staring at a vending machine, trying to look like I have a purpose in this place. And my mind keeps drifting, drifting back, back to that night fourteen years go. The night when I walked in on my father and his secret.

There he was, tangled in off-white bed sheets and another man, both of them slick with the dirty sweat of betrayal.

It was summer, and I always traveled with him when school was out. I never thought to ask why he paid for me to have my own room. Hell, it was an adventure, and what boy doesn't want the freedom to stay up late, eat junk food, and watch tits on cable?

But that night, I'd eaten too many Fritos and Twinkies from the motel vending machine. My stomach hurt; I couldn't sleep. So, I ran to him. My dad. My protector. That wasn't the first time I went to him in the night, but it was the first time his room was unlocked.

The door opened wide and the dominoes tumbled.

I was angry, hurt, confused, and I told everyone what I'd seen. I regret that every day. Every day. But I can't shake the disease. The feeling of betrayal. Of hate.

Mom grabbed us, me and Lily. She took us away from Dad, but not from Sunfall. And our lives turned to shit.

Mom's gone now, living in Des Moines with a new husband, a rich guy that pampers her. We never talk to her, either. She's a different kind of wrong, always was.

Cold. Selfish. And I wonder how much she knew before I opened my big mouth and spilled the poison. My guess is, she knew everything but didn't give a fuck until horror got real with words. Until her pride was bruised. She's like that, one of those people in a state of constant denial, for whom the truth is a lie until it can no longer be denied.

Much as I hate to admit it, I'm not entirely unlike her.

A bag of Fritos stares back at me now, making me feel sick. I punch the vending machine. Hard. Candy bars and breath mints tumble down, and I don't look around. Don't care who might have seen me.

I just walk on, ready as I'll ever be for this moment.

CHAPTER ELEVEN

He looks up from the newspaper and says, "That certainly took long enough."

"I needed time to think," I say.

"Don't you think you've had enough time for that?"

I sit next to him as he folds the paper and puts it on the table.

"Why did you come to me, Jack?" he asks. "Why now?"

"No car," I say. "We needed you."

He shakes his head slowly. "You could have gotten a ride from someone else. You realize that, right?"

"Yeah, well..."

"I want to think you're ready to talk; ready to get it all out and let the past die once and for all. Can we do that?"

"Dad, it's..." I trail off, and he smiles. "I don't know. It's not that simple."

"If it's about my being gay, I—"

"It's never been about that, old man," I snap. "You should know better than that."

"I'm sorry."

"I'm not a bigot."

"Would it have been any worse if you'd caught me with a woman?"

"Are you asking me to retrace my thoughts as a thirteen-year-old boy?"

"If it helps."

"It won't. I've done it too many times to count."

"Then stop."

"Trust me, I'm trying, but what I need to know, *Dad*, is why you married Mom and had a family?"

"It's tough growing up with the way I was—the way I am—in a town like Sunfall. You can either stand outside and get stoned, or you can get with the program. I...well, I got with the program."

I shake my head. "That's not good enough. You had me and Lily. Didn't you love us?"

There's a moment of silence as Dad crosses one leg over the other. He tilts his head back, takes a deep breath, then, tears beating their way out of lidded eyes, he says, "More than anything in the world, Jack. I still see you sometimes, washing cars at Bud Sweeny's. I glimpse your sister around town, too, but...but I just keep moving. Do you know how hard it is for me not to push myself into your lives?"

"Don't think I haven't noticed you. Sunfall's not exactly Los Angeles."

He opens his eyes and nods. "We're just ghosts to each other, aren't we?"

"Something like that."

"I'm not dead, son, not yet, and I still love you and Lily. That's why I stay away from you. Why I don't push.

That's also why I stay here, and why, I want to think, you stay here, too."

"We stay here because we're trapped."

"Keep telling yourself that." There's no accusation in his voice, only sadness.

"Why?" I ask "Why did you take me on those trips?"

"I thought you needed out of the house, son. I wanted to show you the country, and, well, and to get you away from your mother. She went easier on Lil but put way too many demands on you. You were just a kid. You deserved to have a little fun."

"But then, why did you—"

"I didn't mean to. It just... I made a lot of connections in my travels. With people like me, and I was desperate to find something real, to fit in. I was hungry for moments of tenderness and warmth. Intimacy that made sense to me was something I'd been denied for so long."

"I still don't—"

"You're a grown man now. Certainly you know what it means to yearn, to dream, to want something—some*one*— to make you whole. Don't tell me you haven't messed around with the wrong people for the right reasons. We all do."

"I have. But when I think about Nora, when I look at her, my needs, they just vanish. I can't explain it."

"You don't have to. I know what you mean, and I understand why I was so wrong. I'm sorry. I'll apologize a million times if I have to, but you have to understand—"

"I don't *have* to do anything, other than get the hell out of dodge."

"You're leaving?"

"When Lily gets well, we're gone."

"Where?"

"I don't know yet. Somewhere not here."

"Maybe...maybe that's why you came to me now. Did you stop to think about that?"

I hadn't, but it makes a certain amount of sense. Standing, I grab his empty Styrofoam cup. "Looks like you could use a refill," I say.

He nods, wiping tears from his cheeks. "Yeah...thanks."

I turn toward the coffee machine, then stop and spin back to him. "You're right," I say.

He just looks at me, more than a decade of expectation in his eyes.

"I'm not ready to forgive you, Dad, but I don't think it's right that you haven't spent time with your only granddaughter."

"She's a good kid," he says.

"I know. The best."

"She told me what happened. How you stood up to Lily."

"Well," I say, unable to keep the smile from my lips, "she's got a big mouth."

He chuckles, but his expression remains serious. "You're a good man, Jack. You did the right thing. It's hard to stand up to a mother, even when the welfare of her child is at stake. That's just... just a force of nature that no one wants to tangle with."

"Cream and two sugars, right?"

His smile returns, and he says, "Thanks."

I sit with Nora in the backseat. Everyone's quiet, only the sound of the road and Johnny Cash singing about Memphis to keep us company. The man in black sure loved his Tennessee roots. Lucky bastard, that one.

She's just staring out the window, her expression hard to read—a rarity for any child, I suppose, but a downright crime for Nora, who always wears her emotions front and center.

I put my hand on her shoulder and give her a little shake. "You okay, Bear?"

"I am," she says softly. "It just hurt seeing Momma like that." She turns to me. "Did it hurt you, too?"

"A lot," I say.

She considers my face for a moment, seems satisfied with the truth of my words, then nods.

"Everything's going to be all right," I say. "I promise."

Then she hugs me. And everything, everything seems to go back to fine. She's not quaking, not crying. She's just Nora again.

Kids are elastic, quickly snapping back to normal. But, I remind myself, stretch anything too thin and it'll break.

CHAPTER TWELVE

Nora's in the kitchen with Dad, helping him chop vegetables for a salad, and I'm sitting on the couch. The sweet waft of barbecued ribs makes my mouth water as the TV newswoman talks about unrest in the Middle East. Using the remote, I turn the sound down and breathe deep, thinking about what I'd told Dad earlier.

When Lily gets well, we're gone.

So that's it. My mind's made up? Even after taking the money, I still convinced myself that I'd never use ill-gotten gain toward my own purposes. I kept telling myself that I'd donate it to charity or even leave it somewhere for others to find. But when I said that shit to Dad, well...I guess I was finally letting myself in on the truth. While that's putting no case in my marrow, it brings me a certain amount of purpose.

By any means necessary...

Those aren't my words, of course. That's good ol' Malcolm X. He was seeking higher ground, too—even got a little dirty along the way. But I guess, in the end, he found what he was looking for, before a bullet ended him.

Malcolm was born in Nebraska like me. Never talked much about that, at least to my knowledge. Neither did Gerald Ford or Darth Cheney or Johnny Carson. Those guys, they had the sense to leave.

By any means necessary...

The sound of machinegun fire crackles from Dad's console TV, the same set on which, as a kid, I watched news stories from war torn Bosnia. These images of conflict have always been in the background of my life, thousands of miles away — people fighting for their version of right.

The conflict never seems to end. New countries. New faces to call the enemy. But it's all the same. Assholes vs. assholes in the constant game of my god can kick your god's ass.

Back in the '90s, a fair number of Bosnian refugees settled here. I even dated one of 'em in high school. She spoke amazing English, but her folks didn't. I always marveled at how she, at the tender age of sixteen, ran the family. She read the contracts, told her dad what to sign and what not to. She wrote all the goddamn checks. Pretty fucking amazing, that girl. A stone cold bitch, too. That part, I understood. Not a lot of folks around here cut her much slack for that, but I did. As I saw it, she had the intelligence of a forty year old and the emotional capacity of an eight year old.

In the end, she had the sense to get as far away from here as possible. I still think about her sometimes, and I hope she found balance in her life.

Tired of these ruminations, I brush Henrietta from my lap. She mews ruefully, then ambles away as I get up from the couch. Slowly, I pace the living room. High atop bookshelves are Dad's trophies and awards, all of them reminding me that I'm one generation removed from the best goddamn vacuum cleaner peddler the world's ever known. Hard to imagine a time when such a nomadic grift could be a stable, lifelong career.

I scan Dad's many books. Most of the spines are black: Horror, thrillers, some mystery. He was always a fan of the dark stuff, and Mom never let him keep his books in the living room. She was afraid Stephen King would "scare away the company."

Truth was, she did a good enough job of that on her own. She was a lot like the girl I dated back in school. Difference was, she wasn't sixteen, and her life hadn't been shit. As for cutting Mom some slack, can't say I didn't try.

Three books grab my attention. Their author: Charles Lewis.

As I pull them from the shelf, Nora screams. I run for the kitchen, still clutching the books, then breathe a sigh of relief when I see my Bear, doing her best not to cry but otherwise fine. Dad's wrapping her finger in a paper towel, which is lightly splotched with blood.

Nora glances up at me. "I just cut myself," she says.

Dad says, "Not too deep." He notices what I'm holding and says, "Jack, there are some Band-Aids in the bathroom. Can you grab one?"

"Where are they?" I ask.

"Same place as always."

I start for the bathroom, but Dad stops me. "Hey, son," he says. "Can you put those books on the dining room table? They're pretty important to me. Don't want to get blood on them."

"Did you write these?" I ask.

He nods.

All traces of pain leave Nora's face as she looks up at him. "You write books, Grandpa?"

"Something like that," he says.

"Cool," Nora exclaims. She and Dad start talking as I walk into the dining room and set the books on the table.

The cover of the top paperback holds me in place for a moment.

The Darkest Night...

The young man on the cover looks sad. Looks like me when I was a kid. And in the background is a man. The boy's father? Maybe. He doesn't look much like Dad and is wielding a bloody knife. Shivers shuddering through my core, I cringe as I look away.

"What's taking you so long?" Dad calls out.

"Sorry," I say, then I move for the bathroom.

When I open the medicine cabinet, I laugh. These Band-Aids, I remember. *Sesame Street*, featuring images of Big Bird and Cookie Monster. The box is covered in a thick layer of dust, and as I hold it, my mind flashes back. It was summer. I was mowing the lawn; must have been eleven or twelve. The mower spat a rock and laid a deep gash in my arm. I remember Dad frantically opening a box of Band-Aids—this very box—and putting eight or nine of the damn things over the wound, which was pretty awful and gushed blood despite his efforts. He was hysterical, even though Mom couldn't have cared less. He drove me to Seward and got me stitched up, then took me for ice cream.

I look closely at the box. Brush layers of dust away. A dark red stain looks back at me. My blood from a much happier time; a reminder that my dad…he isn't a monster. All too human, yes, but who am I to judge?

I close the medicine cabinet and catch my reflection in the mirror. The man—still a boy in many ways—staring back at me has a secret darker than Dad's. Is this the real reason why I've reached out to him now? My darkness trumping his?

"What're you doing in here?" he says, now standing in the doorway.

"Thinking," I say.

He takes the box from me and studies it for a second, then smirks. "Guess I don't cut myself too often," he says. "Don't guess these things have an expiration date, do they?"

"None that really matters."

Nora steps next to him, holding out her cut finger. Dad kneels down and takes one of the bandages from the box before setting it on the floor. "Okay, Professor," he says, "time to make you good as new." He gently takes the blood-spotted paper towel from her finger.

"Not too bad," Nora says.

"Yes," he agrees. "Not bad at all."

"Cool," she says, admiring the bandage. "*Sesame Street*. You like *Sesame Street*, Grandpa?"

"Of course," he says. "Who doesn't?"

"But…" Confusion peppers her face. "Where's Elmo?"

Dad and I laugh together, and it feels right.

I can easily say this is the best meal I've had in a long time, and I say it often as I eat; so does Nora. Dad thanks us in a modest manner, not a quality I remember from my childhood. Nor do I recall him being a great chef. Most of our meals were Mom's, bland and flavorless, nothing like this. The meat falls from the bone, tender and sweet. The corn on the cob is fresh, which is rare even here in farm country, where the stuff mainly gets harvested for Ethanol and is unfit for human consumption.

I'm three plates of food and four glasses of wine in when the sun starts to set. Full, a little buzzed, and, for the first time in a long time, in a place that shares an area code with something approaching happiness.

Nora dominates the dinner conversation. She wants to know more about Dad's books.

"They're really not books for kids," he says. "But I hope you'll read 'em someday, Professor. I can always use another set of eyes."

"It's funny," she says. "Uncle Jack is always telling me I should be a writer."

"Oh?" Dad says, shifting his attention to me.

"I never knew you wanted to write," I say to him.

"Never knew it myself," he says. "But when Kirby sales went soft, I had to do something." He gestures to the bookshelves. "Surely you remember how much I read."

I take a sip of wine. "All the time."

"You still read a lot?" He asks.

"Yeah," I say. "Non-fiction, mostly."

Dad turns to Nora. "Your Uncle Jack here was interested in everything when he was growing up. Smartest kid ever, and I'm not just saying that 'cause he's mine. Jack here knew more about current events and history and science than most old folks around these parts."

"That's not saying much," I offer with a dismissive wave.

"Uncle Jack's still smart," Nora insists.

"Shame he didn't go to college," says Dad.

I finish off my glass with a gulp and refill it, then I get up and walk across the room to the place where Dad keeps his the books he authored. I grab *The Darkest Night* and open it. Turn to the copyright page, see that the book was published in 2007, then flip to the dedication.

To Jack and Lily, with love.

"Why didn't Uncle Jack go to college?" Nora asks.

"Oh," Dad says, "lots of reasons, I guess."

I skim the first page of prose, immediately impressed; Dad's one hell of a wordsmith, even if the subject's a bit pulpy for my taste.

"This is pretty incredible," I say.

Dad turns to me and laughs. "I had a good editor."

He's being modest again, and I like it. I remember how boastful he used to be on the road. How he called his leads "fresh blood." How he bragged that he could sell ice to an Eskimo. Clichés were a big part of my youth. Anyone who grows up with a salesman for a dad knows what I'm talking about.

I read more. On the page, Dad's not working in clichés. The protagonist, a guy named Rex, takes shape. I already like Rex, and I recognize him as my father. Not the guy I knew, but the man I'm seeing now. Perhaps the man he always yearned to be.

I slide the book back in place and take another long drink of wine.

"It's getting late," Dad says. "And you've been putting the Merlot down pretty fast." He's looking at Nora but talking to me.

"The *Merlot*?" she says.

He picks up her half-empty glass of chocolate milk. "The hard stuff, young lady."

She giggles.

Dad smiles at me and says, "Why don't you two stay here tonight?"

"I don't know," I say.

"Please," Nora whines.

Dad says, "Nora can stay in Lily's old room, and you can stay in yours, Jack."

I walk back to the table. "It is getting late," I agree. "Do you have a toothbrush Nora can use?"

"I think I can rustle one up," Dad says. Then he smiles at Nora. "But you best be getting to bed, Professor."

"Already?" she says.

"Bear," I say, "your grandpa and I need to talk."

I skim Dad's books while he stares at the ceiling. Nora went down fast, which wasn't a surprise; today, after all, was long for her.

"I have more copies out in the garage," he says, "if you want your own."

I hold up the book, his second, published in 2009, *The Waking Hole*. "I thought you said these were special?"

"They are," he says. "Those are the ARCs, the first print copies of my books. I have boxes and boxes of mass-markets, which are actually of better construction."

I put the book down on the end table and say, "I'm impressed. I really am."

He shrugs, goes back to looking at the ceiling. After a long moment of doing this, he looks at me and says, "We create our environment."

"Huh?"

"I've been trying to think of the right thing to say, and that's all I could come up with. Not very good, is it?"

"And here you are, the writer."

He doesn't laugh; instead, his serious expression deepens. "Here's what I mean. Running away solves nothing. Is that a little more...clear?"

"It makes more sense," I say, "but I don't know I'd — "

"Son," he says. "There's a cloud hanging over you. I don't know what it is, but I know it's there. You can fool a lot of people, even your niece, but I learned your body language pretty well in your first thirteen years. So what is it?"

"No."

"No, what?"

"You don't get to do this. Not like this. I'm back in your life for one day and you're trying to psychoanalyze me already. No."

"I'm sorry, I — "

"I've got problems, Dad. I've got a lot of problems, okay? And I've been trying to solve those problems here, been trying to help Bud Sweeny by making off-the-clock sales pitches for him."

Dad smiles. "You've been trying to crack into sales?"

"How 'bout that, huh? A chip off the old block."

"Son, selling shit isn't what it used to be. People around here don't have much money, and you don't sell cars by cold calling. People, they know where the lot is."

I close my eyes and take a deep breath. "I know, Dad. Like I said, I've been trying to solve my problems here, but…but that isn't working."

"Do you want to go to school? Is that it? I still have every penny of your college fund. Hell, I even add to it when I can. Lily's, too. It's never too late."

"I don't want your money."

"It's not mine," he says. "It's yours. It's always been yours."

"No."

"What's wrong with you? — why won't you take — "

"Mom kicked me out of the house when I was eighteen, Dad. You were off limits. I didn't qualify for loans, so that chapter is closed in my life, and I have to move on."

"I don't under — "

"I'm thinking about Nora now. And Lily. I want to get them out of here so they can prosper. Someplace with work, any kind of work. It's not about breaking into sales; it's about making an honest living. I want Nora to have a chance."

"But Nora's not the one with the cloud over her head."

Maybe he's right. Perhaps I'm full of shit.

No. Sunfall is the disease, with its decrepit roads and buildings, what few we have; with its bigmouth residents and lack of jobs. I don't create the environment here. I'm not the fucking chamber of commerce. So I shake my head and say, "You have a point, Dad, but what I'm doing, really trying to do, is prevent that cloud from ever finding her."

He gets up from his chair. "I'm going to bed," he says. "Your room's waiting for you, just like you left it."

"If it's all right with you," I say, "I'd rather sleep on the couch tonight."

"Fine with me. Can I ask why?"

"I don't know. It's just...I've confronted the past enough for one day. I don't regret it, honestly, but I don't want to overdo it, either. Does that make sense?"

Dad clenches my shoulder with a firm grip. "It does," he says. His grip tightens. "Do me a favor, okay?"

"What is it?" I ask.

"Don't leave without saying goodbye. Everyone deserves goodbye."

"I won't. I promise."

He pats me hard on the back then heads down the dark hallway to his room.

CHAPTER THIRTEEN

I'm not really sleeping when my cell starts chirping, but I'm trying. Much as I'd like to say spending the night in my boyhood home brings back moments of comfort, that's just not where my head's at.

The first two calls roll to voicemail. But when the third beckons, I reach into my jeans pocket and snatch the phone, ready to turn it off, looking at the azure display.

Incoming Call... Unknown...

"Goddamn," I whisper. It's either Lee or the hospital. Either way, it can't be good news. If it's Lee, I need to know he's away from here. If it's the hospital, I need to know everything's all right. "Hello," I say.

"Did I wake you up, amigo?"

"Yeah, what is it? You in Chicago yet?" I whisper.

"No," he says, and the fear in his voice makes me sit up straight.

"What's wrong?" I ask.

"Have you been watching the news?"

"Not really, why?"

"Why are you whispering?"

"Nora's asleep."

"Oh, okay. Hey, that phone of yours—it's a *burner*, right?"

"What's that?"

"A tract phone, prepaid, not under your name."

"Yeah."

"Good."

"What the hell's going on?"

"867-5309," he says.

"What are you talking about? You want me to call that number?"

"Jenny, Jenny," he drones, and I suddenly remember the old Tommy Tutone tune.

"What about her?"

"Turns out that little Jenny Snowdon had a rich daddy in Cali. This thing has become a media circus. They're offering a quarter-mil reward for any information leading to her killer. Feds might even get involved. Might *be* involved."

My heart races. "What?" I swallow the lump in my throat. "What do you want me to do, Lee?"

"You spend any money, honey?"

"No."

"Good."

"Why haven't you left town?"

"And what, become suspect number one? No, bro. People know my plans—that I'm not supposed to be shoving off just yet. If I shift gears too quick, might send up a few red flags. Can't do that, cat."

"You sound...you sound paranoid." *And drunk.*

"Maybe. Maybe not. If it keeps me out of federal lockup, I'll risk a bit of sanity. Really wasn't looking for this shit to cross state lines."

"Fuuuck. They had California plates, asshole. What did you think—"

"I need you to do something, amigo."

"What the fuck do you want from me? I'm done with—"

"Bring the money to me in front of the DQ."

"Now? Are you—"

"Bring it to me, and we'll decide what to do with it."

"This is crazy. You told me that—"

"Bring it to me, then we'll go for a little ride. I've got a plan for where we can hide it until this thing blows over. A small town like this?—they can just go around issuing warrants on everyone's cracker asses. And they're gonna start with the poorest, the most desperate. Tag, you're it."

"And you didn't see this coming before?"

"Nope. Thought the bitch and her boy were some kinda wanna-be Bonnie and Clyde."

"I'll bring you the money," I say, "but you're gonna hide it on your own, and I don't want anything to do with this anymore."

"Just meet me, amigo."

"Fuck you."

"Hey, I'm just looking out for our asses."

"Fuck you," I repeat, then hang up the phone.

I get up from the couch and clutch my screaming head, no idea what to do next. Lee's probably already been to my place, otherwise he wouldn't have called. If I don't show, he'll put two and two together and eventually end up here. That, I can't allow. That'd fuck my whole world for real.

Desperate, I walk to Dad's desk and open the top left hand drawer. And there it sits, just like it always has (except when he was on the road). Dad's .38 Special.

I grab the gun and study it. Fuck, I hate these things. Dad took me to the shooting range as a kid, but I stopped going. Even Mom thought I was a pussy. But I remember how to load the gun, and I remember how it works. So I close the drawer and open the one below it. This is where Dad keeps the bullets. Never understood that. Here's his desk, not four feet from the front door. Gun unloaded. Bullets in a completely separate place. And yet he always claimed he kept the gun for self-defense? Bullshit. Folks around here just like guns, plain and simple. Talking and guns and college football: a real mecca for humanity. Could be something in the water, and maybe that's why I always avoid the tap.

Rather than load the chamber here, I slide the gun and six bullets into my front pocket. Then, as quietly as I can, I unlock the front door and press into the muggy summer night.

CHAPTER FOURTEEN

I don't plan to kill Lee, and I'm not bringing him the money. The gun's purpose is twofold: self-defense, of course, but it's also a threat. My pleas have so far fallen on deaf ears, so it's time, much as I hate it, to lay down the law.

When I get to the DQ, Lee's car isn't in the lot, but I keep walking. He's around here somewhere, I know, and I'm staying strong. Not letting him maintain the upper hand. Once in the parking lot, I look around and say, "Where are you?"

High beams suddenly come alive in Bud Sweeny's lot, and I shield my eyes against the familiar glare of Lee's headlamps. He steps out of the car and motions for me to approach, but I shake my head and gather my courage. Here he is, changing the rules again.

No. Not this time.

"Cut the lights, Lee," I say, moving across the west side wall of the "Brazier," whatever the fuck that means. Then I add, "Come to me."

"You brought the money?"

"Come here," I growl.

Finally, he cuts the lights and struts across the lot. Getting closer, he says, "I didn't want to stand out like a sore thumb, so I thought it was best to park with other cars."

"Yeah," I say, "you're a fucking genius."

"What's wrong with you, Jack?" He halts his advance. "Why are you busting my balls?"

Almost to the back of the building now, I say, "You don't want to look suspicious, right?"

"Yeah."

"Well, let's talk behind the fucking building then. If a cop drives by, we don't end up on their radar."

"Inside the car, moving, that's the safe place to be, amigo."

"Come here," I repeat, and he starts walking.

I slide the revolver, which I loaded on the way over, out of my pocket and wait in the shadows for Lee to round the corner. When he does, I grab him by the neck, pull him close, and jam the barrel of the gun hard into his temple.

"Jesus Christ," he cries.

"It's fucking loaded, douchebag, and don't think I won't fire. Blow your brains all over this wall. Is that what you want, bitch?"

"What the hell has —"

"Shut up!" I let go of him, but the gun remains steady on its target. With my free hand, I pat him down.

"Where's your gun, Lee?"

"In my car, under the seat."

"That where you *always* keep it?"

"Yeah."

"So why did you have it your pants the other night when we were checking on the other car?"

"You never know what to expect when you're dealing with strangers."

"You know, I bet Jenny Snowdon would agree with you on that count."

I push him, and he takes a stumble-step away from me. He looks like he's going to run, so I say, "Stop there," and he does. "Now, kneel on the ground and listen to me."

"You've lost your mind, Jack," he pleads. "You're not thinking right."

Motioning to the ground with the gun, I repeat, "Kneel."

Slowly, he crouches, drops one knee to the pavement, then the other. The look on his face is priceless. Pure fear, just like the shit he planted behind my eyes, the permanent stain he left in my brain. In this moment, I'm not so sure I want to let him live. Should he live, I hope the rest of his days are haunted by this—that this shit sends ripples through his family line, letting them know not to fuck with me or mine.

"What do you want?" Lee whimpers, sounding like a child now. Like the kid I knew back in grade school; the little redheaded, freckle-faced, snot-nosed freak that kids called "Stinky Lee."

"You know what I want," I say.

Lee's crying now.

"I want you to leave me alone. I don't care where you go, but get out of town and don't come back."

"And..and what if I get caught, Jack? Are you thinking about that?"

"No, and I don't want to."

"But—"

"You're sly, you're resourceful. So don't get caught."

"What about—"

"Here's the plan," I say slowly. "You take care of Lee, and I take care of me. Got it?"

He nods, tears running down his reddened face.

"You fuck with me one more time, asshole," I say, "and I'll fucking kill you. I won't hesitate."

"Come on, Jack. You can't do me like this."

I laugh, but there's no joy in the gesture. "You've got to be kidding. Who the hell brought us here, huh? Three days ago, I was trying to put my life together, then you show up and manage to fuck me all the way to kingdom come."

"I didn't mean—"

"Fuck you," I say. "You never mean to fuck me, but you always do."

"I—"

"Fuck you."

"I—"

I stride at Lee and press the revolver into his forehead. "Say 'I' one more time and I'll fucking kill you."

Silence ensues, only the sounds of our heavy breathing and the crickets to keep us company.

Finally, I pull the gun away from his head and say, "Is my message clear?"

"Crystal."

"We've been through a lot together, Lee. I remember how kids picked on you, how I was your only friend, how I defended you."

"I know, man, and I love you for it."

"But you went bad anyway, didn't you?—went bad and always tried to drag me down with you."

"I'm sorry."

"You made yourself tough, learned how to fight, to scrap, to survive—I respected that. Still do. But you've crossed the line one too many times."

I aim the gun at him again, and this time I press the trigger.

Click.

A wet blotch spreads down the legs of Lee's khakis, and he's balling now.

"The other five chambers are loaded," I say. "Want me to squeeze again?"

"Please don't kill me, Jack. I promise, promise I'll leave—I'll get out of town. I promise."

"Your word and nickel are worth five cents," I say.

"I promise," he bawls. "I promise."

"Know this, Lee, I hate you. I've hated you for a long time."

"I'll go, just don't kill me."

"To me," I say, "you're already dead."

Then I turn my back on Lee and start for his car. When I get there, I pop open the door, snatch his Glock from beneath the seat, and start jogging back to Dad's.

Fueled by adrenaline, I'm moving faster than I have in a long time. The dark within dark night bounces in my sweat-streaked vision, and my pulse thrums like the rhythm section of a heavy metal band.

Halfway between Main Street and Dad's, I stop. Breathing deeply, I clutch my knees, bent over, nauseous. Then I throw up, and Dad's barbecue, it doesn't taste as good the second time.

Everything spins, spots multiplying in my periphery. Then, sight balancing, I see two yellow eyes staring at me from the darkness, the shape around those eyes slowly bleeding into focus.

It's the black dog. The Labrador. The one I'd fed then assumed dead. It's still scrawny and sad, but not dead. Just staring at me, probably hoping I've got some burgers in my pockets.

"Sorry, boy," I say.

A curious tilt of its head, then the dog sniffs my vomit and starts eating.

FRIDAY

CHAPTER FIFTEEN

I'm trying to push the image of that damn vomit-eating dog out of my head, and here's Dad, frying bacon and singing along with some country-western radio station out of Lincoln. The scent of food and fresh-brewed coffee is doing nothing to heal me, and Willie Nelson, or whoever the hell is twanging away, is about to push me over the edge. But I hold my shit in check, 'cause sitting across the table from me, staring inquisitively, is Nora.

"You don't look so good," she says.

Closing my eyes, I rub my head. "Don't feel so hot, either."

Dad walks into the dining room and sets a steaming plate of bacon and eggs in the middle of the table. "Eat up," he says.

"None for me," I say.

He regards my apathy with a grunt, but Nora starts piling food onto her plate. "I'm gonna get fat if I keep eating here," she says, then pours herself a big glass of orange juice.

Now that the food is closer to me, I wince, and my stomach does somersaults.

"You didn't drink *that* much last night, did you?" Dad says.

"Might be a bug," I say, grabbing my gut.

Dad turns to Nora. "Hey, Professor, your Uncle Jack and I are gonna step outside for a minute, okay?"

Still chowing down, she nods, not really paying attention to either of us.

Listlessly, I get up and follow Dad through the kitchen. He grabs a steaming mug from next to the sink then keeps on walking. Through the porch door. Onto the back deck. He takes a sip of coffee, then reaches into his shirt pocket and pulls out a pack of Kools.

"You quit when I was a kid," I say.

"Well, you're still a kid, and once a smoker always a smoker." He lights the cigarette and takes a deep drag.

"Can I get one of those?" I ask.

"Not you, too."

"Quit a few months ago for Nora, but…"

"But you still sneak one every once in a while. You're preaching to the choir." Dad hands me a cigarette then lights it for me. We stand there for a while, looking at each other and smoking, then he asks, "So, where did you go last night?"

"Heard me, huh?" I'm trying to act casual while my mind races around for a lie. Dad, he just nods, then takes another deep drag. "I couldn't sleep," I say. "Went for a walk."

"Do you always take a gun on your walks?"

"No, I—"

"Don't lie to me, son. That gun and her ammo haven't moved more than a centimeter in the better part of a decade. Might be getting old, and I don't care if you call me a little OCD, 'cause I am, but I know when someone's been rooting through my shit."

"I'm sorry, Dad, but—"

"You're in trouble, I can tell."

"Not anymore, Dad. Everything's square now. I promise. I didn't shoot the gun."

"Yeah, I know. All the bullets are accounted for, and the thing hasn't been fired—I'd be able to tell if it had."

"I just thought I needed it for protection."

"Protection against what? Who? What the hell have you—"

"I'd rather not say."

"Goddamn—"

"Just trust me, okay?"

"I'm trying."

"Good. I can't ask for more than that."

"You shouldn't even be asking for that."

"I know." I turn away from Dad and study the backyard. It seemed so big when I was kid. Now, it looks small. Sprinklers sputter water into the lush grass. Nearby, a hummingbird eats from a hanging feeder. Dad's small patch of paradise, same as it ever was.

You make your own environment…

That sure is true for the old man.

In my mind, I imagine the old swing set where it used to be, and Lily pushing me, her younger brother. We're both smiling. *"Higher, Lil,"* I would shout. *"Higher. Higher."*

Now, here I am, so very low. Out of excuses. Running on fumes.

"Dad," I say.

He doesn't respond, just keeps puffing on his Kool.

"Why didn't you just leave Mom before things got out of hand? I don't think she would have put up much of a fight."

"Because," he says, tone sad, "I loved her."

I spin to face him, and the lie I expect to see on his face registers as truth.

"I loved her," he repeats. "Still do."

"How?"

"You love Nora don't you?"

"Sure, but—"

"Love and sex don't have anything to do with each other. You get that when you're young. You get it again when you're old. But somewhere in between, folks, they just sorta lose sight of simple truths when their hormones run amok. It's how we're wired. People talk about 'being in love,' as if that label means anything. Folks even qualify love as something like 'love you as a friend.' But, fact is, love is *love*. Sex, that's a whole different bug."

"So…?"

"So, I love your mom, always will. More importantly, I loved us. Always wanted a family, but my biology, my *sex* side, wanted something else. Tried to have my cake and eat it, too. Nowadays, gay men can live more normal lives. We can marry in some places, adopt children. That's good. Puts our biology in line with our ideals. But that luxury didn't exist for me."

"I understand."

"Hope so, but it doesn't matter if you do or you don't. All that matters is love."

"Do you have anyone?"

"I don't know. What about you?"

"Have a date on Saturday night. Does that count?"

"Do you love her?"

"Just met her."

"Well, then it counts for something, maybe, but it'll count a lot more when there's love."

I field strip my cigarette butt and throw the debris into the yard. Dad does the same.

"I'd buy an ashtray," he says, "but then I'd have to admit that I'm really a smoker."

"Are you mad at me, Dad?" I ask.

"Just disappointed. Not mad."

"We gotta take this slow."

"Can you and Nora stay for a while? A few days longer? I feel safer with you here."

"We're not much protection."

"No. I feel like it's safer for you and her."

There's no arguing with that, so I don't. "Sure, Dad. We'll stick around."

"I can take Nora shopping later, get her some new clothes so you don't have to take her back to Lily's."

"Thanks."

He lights another cigarette and turns away from me, now looking into the yard. His eyes follow movements that aren't there, and I wonder what ghosts he's seeing.

CHAPTER SIXTEEN

While Dad's shopping with Nora in Grand Island, I head over to my apartment. Lee's gun is cold against my back, stuffed in the band of my jeans, and the fact that I'm carrying the murder weapon isn't lost on me. I don't plan to hold onto it much longer, if I can help it, but I'm not ready to lose the gun just yet; not until I know it won't be needed.

When I get to my front door, I instantly notice that the wood around the deadbolt is splintered. Not happy to see this, but I'm not particularly surprised. I push the door open slowly as I slide the Glock out of my pants.

"Lee," I say, "you here?"

I sweep the living room and the bedroom, but there's no sign of him. I look under the bed. The money, of course, is gone, and that includes the five hundred plus change I'd stashed away honestly. I sit on the edge of the futon, shaking my head. And despite Lee's final betrayal, taking something that was rightfully mine, I'm strangely relieved. After all, he had four hundred dollars of that money coming, and a hundred and change is a small price to pay for absolution.

Then I look at the gun in my palm, and that word—absolution—it just withers and dies. There's none of that for me; never will be. Whatever happens from here, Jenny Snowdon will haunt me for the rest of my days.

I put the gun down on my night table then snatch the phone book from the floor. I flip through the thin white pages and quickly locate the number for Lee's grandmother.

Four rings, then an old frail voice answers.

"Is Lee there?" I ask.

"No. He's not. Can I ask who's calling?"

"This is Jack Lewis, his old friend."

"Oh, Jacky Boy, how are you?"

"Fine. How are you?"

"Old," she says flatly, then laughs. "Not much fun, I'll tell ya."

"Do you know when Lee will be back?" I ask.

"Well," she says, as if she's just been asked the million dollar question on a game show. "Well, he packed up this morning and said he was off to make his fortune, so…"

"So, he already left town."

"Sure did. Heck, you know how that boy is. Hard to pin him down, that one."

Swept up in a wave of relief, I laugh at her observation. "Sure is."

"He does talk about you a lot, Jack. You was about the only real friend that boy ever had 'round here."

"Next time you see him, will you tell him something for me?"

"Let me get a pen..." Before I can tell her not to worry about it, a series of clatters fill the line, followed by a period of silence. Finally, after an abrupt *thunk*, she says, "Shoot it at me."

Looking at the gun, I cringe at her choice of words. "Just tell him I don't really hate him."

"That all?"

"Yes ma'am."

"All right then, sure he'll be glad to hear it. Next time he's around you should let me cook for you boys."

"That sounds nice." I end the call with a series of pleasantries then grab the gun. Walking for the bathroom, I discharge the clip. Then I snatch a clean hand towel from below the sink, wrap the gun in it, and methodically wipe the weapon free of prints. I lay the gun on the sink, careful not to touch it, then I wipe down the clip. After I'm satisfied, having cleaned both items for more than twenty minutes, I slide the clip back into gun, careful not to touch it directly, then wrap the weapon in the towel.

The walk to Cromwell's Pond on Farm Road 19 takes more than thirty minutes, but I can't risk potential lookie loos. Old people in Sunfall, they tend to sit in front of their windows, and anything a notch above slow-drying paint has a way of becoming gossip.

Now at the pond, I let the gun slide from the towel.

Plop.

I wad the blue towel and stuff it in my back pocket, then I kneel before the shimmering green water, tears streaming down my face, my reflection a haggard imitation of my better self, the self I've never really been and hope to one day meet, and whisper, "I'm sorry, Jenny."

Back at Dad's, I finally watch the news. I listen to the desperate, tearful pleas of Lyle Snowdon.

And I cry a lot more.

Unable to stomach more misery, I head to the garage. I grab Dad's tool kit and a container of wood putty, then walk to my apartment and fix the broken door.

And still, I cry.

It's a little after seven when Nora and Dad get home. Nora's excited about all her new clothes, trying on outfits for Dad, doing little fairy dances around the living room. Her happiness brings some comfort, but I'm not really there for it.

Pulling Dad aside, I say, "I need to be alone tonight."

Understanding lights his eyes, for which I'm thankful. "We're going over to Seward in a little bit to see Lily," he says.

"Best I don't go," I say. "I'll only be used to run defense, and I think it's important you talk to her."

With that, I start toward my old bedroom, Henrietta following close at my heels. Before I disappear down the hallway, Nora stops me, twirling around in a baby blue summer dress. "Don't you just love this blue?" she asks with a smile.

Leaning against a wall, I smile and say, "Uncle Jack's gonna need to be alone tonight, okay?"

"You're tired, aren't you?"

I laugh, not just for her benefit but because of her ability to see simple truths. "It's the most beautiful shade of blue in the world, Bear."

She hugs me tightly as I prepare to walk into the past. And in that moment, that one simple moment, I'm awake once more.

Awake and ready.

So it's not with tears that I walk into my old room. Not with the burden of despair that I stare at old family photographs and friends now lost to the tyranny of clocks.

It's with hope. Hope for a new and better tomorrow.

Around eight-thirty, the sun still shining like an angry god, I lie in my old single bed, pull the covers over my head, snuggle a pillow close to my face, and let myself dream. Dream about Paige.

Less than a minute later, I'm asleep.

SATURDAY

CHAPTER SEVENTEEN

I arrive on the lot early, thinking I can get started before Bud gets into the office, hoping that I can get off before five to get ready for my date with Paige. To my surprise, Bud's already there, standing outside his office, wearing, in addition to a spiffy hat of some bygone era, a suit that actually looks like it was tailored in this century.

"Can you step into my office?" he asks in a hauntingly official manner.

The air conditioner rattles and papers do a slow dance on Bud's desk. Lighting a cigarette, he leans back in his chair and motions for me to sit.

"What's wrong?" I ask, taking the seat across from him.

"Wife's sister in Omaha went and died on Wednesday," he says without emotion. "Never cared much for that busy-body bitch, but Brenda's a wreck over the whole mess." He takes off his hat, puts it on the desk, then runs a hand through his thinning red-gray hair.

"Sorry to hear that."

"Funeral's today," he says, "which is why I'm all gussied up."

"No worries, Bud, I can take the day—"

"How serious are you about selling cars?" He leans across the desk, staring at me, through me, his bullshit detector turned past ten.

I take a deep breath and say, "Very," pushing hard into his gaze, forcing myself not to blink.

Bud smiles and leans back as he takes a drag from his Pall Mall. Smoke serpents swirl around his head. "You know the routine. We finance through First Confederated across the street." He hands me a credit application. "Most important thing on there is the Social. Get as much as you can, but don't let them leave the Social Security Number blank. Fax it to the number on the top and they'll give you a yes or no."

"Bank's closed today, Bud."

"The faxes route into a call center on Saturdays. Response time is actually a hell of a lot faster, believe it or not."

"Okay."

"Answer comes back yes, you give 'em the keys and make sure they drive off the lot. Comes back no, you give 'em the bad news. Hate to say this, but the bad news is likely all you'll be giving." He hands me a triplicate form. "Here's the contract. Make sure every field is filled out, and make sure they sign it. Don't worry about titles or anything; I'll process that shit on Monday. Not that I think they'll be anything to process."

"What if they want to pay cash?"

Bud laughs. "Son," he says, "no one pays in cash anymore." Then he scribbles something on a piece of paper and slides it across the desk. "But if some Rockefeller wants to buy one of my beauties, call me here and I'll walk you through the paces. Easy peasy Japanesey."

"No problem."

"You know where the temp tags are. Folks 'round here are no-joke broke so give 'em thirty days, and be sure to slap one inside the front and back window." As he's saying this, Bud grabs his hat and starts for the door.

I spin my chair and ask, "What about margins? Wiggle room?"

Laughing, he keeps moving, then, before stepping outside, he puts his hat back on and turns to me. "I know you look at the books, Jack. Just follow my lead."

"Fair enough," I say, unsuccessfully fighting the flush that's rushing my face.

"And don't get nervous. Hell, if you actually sell something today, I'll eat my hat."

"Better bring some ketchup on Monday." I put on my best smile. "Might help that thing go down a little easier."

With a dismissive wave and a dry chuckle, he says, "Oh, I almost forgot," and fishes a cluster of keys from his front pocket. I approach him as he untangles a key from the chain. "Lock up for a few minutes," he says, "then head home and put on something a little more...professional. Open up when you look respectable."

"Suit and tie?" I ask, taking the key from him.

With more than a trace of disbelief, he asks, "You have a suit?"

"Yes."

Rapidly nodding as he steps through the door, Bud says, "That'll do."

While the kid is admiring the Korean sports car, I pull his father, my old high school track coach, aside. "Mike," I say, "that's the car your son seems to want."

"What can you tell me about it, Jack?"

"She's fast, has high miles, and the last kid that drove her is lucky to be alive."

Mike Mitchell laughs. "Interesting sales tactic."

With a smile, I say, "Come here," then—Mike's son still ogling the Tiburon—I lead him over to a Chevy Cavalier. "This," I say, "is the car you *want* to buy."

"What year?"

"'98."

"Little old, don't you think?"

Opening the door of the coupe, I invite Mike to have a seat. "Fifty thousand original miles on the engine," I say. "Was owned by Bea Lumley, and she drove it to church once a week in Seward. Regular oil changes, well taken care of. Best of all, it's a four cylinder, which means your boy's less likely to wrap it around a telephone pole."

Looking around the dash, Mike says, "No CD player. Rick isn't going to like that."

"The first thing he'll want to modify is the stereo, no matter what's in the dash. Question is, you buying your boy his first car or his tenth stereo?"

Mike keeps laughing.

"Reliable transportation," I say, "safe, and…it'll cost you half what that Korean bullet will."

"You know we're just window shopping today, don't you?"

"You mentioned that. Planning to head into Lincoln later and check the lots there, you said."

"That's right."

"Might be able to save a couple hundred bucks that way, but here's the difference."

"Hit me, I'm all ears." Really, he's all smile, and about a thousand miles from buying anything.

"You know who owned this car. You know she didn't abuse it. Also, you buy this car, your money stays here in Sunfall. Lincoln takes care of Lincoln, Mike. Times like these, a man has to ask, who's taking care of *us*?"

Mike stops laughing, his look suddenly serious, and I'm not sure whether he's getting ready to hit me or leave. Instead, he sticks out his hand. I take it. We shake. Two men. Eyes locked. "You're right," he says in a deep, serious voice. "You're absolutely right."

Five minutes later, we're in the office.

Thirty minutes later, the late Bea Lumley's Cavalier leaves the lot with Rick Mitchell, happy as he'll ever be, behind the wheel.

A little before three, the phone rings.

"How's the place holding up?" Bud asks.

"It's still here," I say, trying not to sound too cocky.

"Well?"

"Ran a couple bad credit applications. Terry Lawrence and Marty Jasper."

"Usual suspects," Bud says. "How'd they take the news?"

"Like they expected it."

"Sounds about right."

"And I sold a car to Mike Mitchell."

"Lucky break, kid. His son's been eyeing that Tiburon for weeks. Knew it was only a matter of time before—"

"Sold him the '98 Cav."

"Bea Lumley's old car? Been trying to move that thing for two years."

"I know."

"How'd you—"

"I reasoned with the decision maker instead of playing the kid's game."

Bud laughs. "Goddamn, you might just have the stuff after all. What'd you get?"

"Full price."

More laughter. "Well, if that doesn't beat all. Hey, I'm heading back into town now—let me take you out for a steak. We can talk about the future."

"Can't, I have a date."

"A date, huh? Sounds like I really underestimated you."

"Just a little."

"Lock up and have a good time—you've earned it."

"Thanks."

"Oh, and can you come in on Monday morning?"

"Sure."

"We'll talk more then."

CHAPTER EIGHTEEN

When I get back to my apartment to pick up clothes, there's a note taped to my mail box.

What the hell happened to my door?!?!
Ernie

Heading inside, I ball up the message and toss it at the trashcan in the kitchen. A real three point shot and then some. The paper ball sails...sails...bounces off the rim...lands in the can...

...and the crowd goes wild!

"Fuck you, Ernie," I mutter. Then, laughing like a kid, I jaunt to my closet and grab my finest digs.

At Dad's, Nora sits on the porch swing with a thousand yard stare. After a long moment of me standing on the porch, she acknowledges my presence. "Hi, Uncle Jack."

There's no sadness in her voice, just fatigue. Putting my free hand on the swing's chain, I sit next to her.

"You look nice today," she says. "Is that suit for your date?"

"The suit's for work." I hold up the stack of clothes—a burgundy Perry Ellis oxford and a pair of charcoal gray slacks.

With a look of surprise, she says, "You washed cars in *that*?"

"Not today. Today I *sold* cars."

"That sounds like fun."

"It was. Where's Dad? Why are you out here alone?"

"He's inside talking to Momma. They didn't tell me to go outside, but I kinda thought it was best to give 'em some space, you know."

"That's…that's probably best. I didn't think she'd be out of the hospital for a while."

"There was a problem with her 'surance. Grandpa yelled at the lady behind the desk, then he offered to pay for everything, but Momma wouldn't let him do it. Said she'd be all right."

"How are they getting along?"

"Who?"

"Your mom and grandpa, who else?"

"Well…"

I give her enough time to answer, then nudge with, "Yes?"

"I don't know," she says. "They're not yelling, but…I'd prolly be inside if it felt all right. I mean, *The Flintstones* is on TV. My favorite one, too."

Quickly remembering the episode in question, I adopt a pseudo-serious expression. "'You, sir, are a wiggly worm.'"

Her eyes go wide as she laughs. "Princestone University," she bellows. "I love it."

"Ah, you have that on DVD anyway. You can watch it whenever."

"Yeah, but I like it best when the TV plays it. Makes me feel less...crazy."

This spins me. "What do you mean?"

"Well, kids at school call the stuff I watch 'lame.' They say it's 'old' and 'stupid.' Say that *Flintstones* are just dumb vitamins. But when the TV plays it, I feel like...like someone's agreeing with me, you know."

"I agree with you."

"Sure, but you're my Uncle Jack. You have to agree with me 'cause you love me. The person at the TV station who plays my show doesn't even know me."

"Huh," I say. "That's...that's an interesting point."

"So, you nervous 'bout your date with Paige?"

Rather than answer with words, I hold up two slightly separated fingers.

"Do you," Nora says, "*love* her?"

Putting my arm around her shoulder, I laugh. "I don't even know her yet."

"But you want to, don't you?"

"Very much."

"Will she come with us when we leave?"

"I don't know. Probably not."

"Why?"

"Well, there's just not enough time to..."

"Why?"

I pull her close. "Aren't we getting ahead of ourselves?"

"You tell me."

"I think I just did."

We sit there for a while, not saying anything, and I, sweating up a storm in my wool suit, start longing for the air-conditioned comfort of Dad's house.

Finally, Nora breaks the silence: "If you start to love her, will you stop loving me?" She looks up with the most heartbreaking eyes I've ever seen.

"Why would you ask that?"

"I don't know. It just crossed my mind."

"No, of course not. I'll never stop loving my Bear."

"Never hurts to ask."

As I stand and start for the door, Nora says, "Uncle Jack?"

I turn. "Yeah."

"'You, sir, are a wiggly worm,' and I'll never stop loving you, too."

Chuckling, I step inside, but my mirth quickly withers. Lily's asleep on the couch, and Dad's sitting next to her in a chair, just staring at her.

"I don't understand," he whispers, "how someone can do this kind of thing to another human being." He turns to me, eyes red.

"She never did know how to run away from trouble."

Dad stands up and walks toward me. "But *you* do?"

Looking down at the carpet, I shake my head. "No. But I'm learning."

"Heard you talking to Nora through the window. So, Bud let you work the lot, huh?"

"Yeah."

"Well...?"

Teeming with pride, I say, "Made my first sale."

He manages a brief smile, then says, "Sometimes, son, it's better not to walk away."

"Dad, I need to—"

"Listen to me." Dad pulls some cash out of his pocket—three twenties—and hands it to me. "This is for your date tonight. Have a good time. But remember, sometimes it's better *not* to walk away."

"Thanks," I whisper.

"I love you," he says.

"Thanks again." Then, without another word, I head to the bathroom.

CHAPTER NINETEEN

The fabric of my life isn't sewn with many moments beyond articulation. Don't suppose too many lives are. But only one word fits Paige as she saunters across the street to meet me.

Grace.

Her pink sundress flutters in the boiling breeze, and she's wearing her strawberry hair up. Red lips. Smokey eyes. And the way she moves: catlike but on the safe side of sultry; confident but far from smug.

Like I said: grace.

Smiling, she doesn't approach like a stranger, like so many have on first dates. Familiarity. That's a big part of this; hard to explain, but easy on the eyes and the soul.

We start with a hug, not a handshake. She instigates, but me, I'm not complaining.

"You look nice," she says.

"I clean up pretty well," I respond with a chuckle. "You...I really don't have words for you."

She twirls around once, beautifully childlike, then says, "What, this old thing?"

I take her hand and we start walking. For a few seconds, I worry she can feel my nerves through the vibrations of my grip, but then I realize, I can feel hers. There's comfort in that.

"You look wonderful," I say. "Just so there's no confusion about—"

"Why would there be any confusion," she says. "I saw the answer in your eyes. The eyes, they talk for us when we don't have words."

We do that a lot, Paige and I, we talk without talking. This, I know, is *us*. Silence in my life is routinely a story of discomfort, but not now. Not with her. She puts salad in my bowl, and I like that. The simplicity of it. Of *us*. The little things, like the way she sips her wine. The way she compliments the waitress about the food, even though the truth is in her eyes. The food is bland. Everything in Sunfall is. But not Paige. She's a breath of fresh air, a blast of oxygen in the driest desert. And the truth, it's not hidden from me. It's all there. Her life has been tough, I can see. One disappointment after another.

Our entrees are consumed, wine glasses empty, and I'm talking about Nora. I've been talking a lot about her, maybe too much, but a twinkle in Paige's eye tells me something important.

"How old's your child?" I ask.

"I never told you I have a child," she says, smiling.

"How old?" I'm not pressing. The smile, I'm wearing it, too. And my voice, it's gentle. How could anyone ever dare raise their voice to this angel?

"He's nine."

"What's his name?"

"Cody."

"How was everything?" That's the waitress checking in on us. I affirm that everything is terrific, because it is, before ordering more wine. First I check Paige's eyes, making sure that's what she really wants. She does. I order the wine. The waitress walks away.

Paige leans across the table, eyes intense, cutting but not injuring. "Talking without talking," she says.

"What are my eyes telling you right now?"

"They tell me you're a good guy, mostly. But they say something dark, too."

"Like what?"

She shrugs and leans back. "I'm not psychic," she says. "But...but I don't think there's anything there I can't handle. Also, you want to kiss me."

Now it's my turn to lean forward. She follows my lead. And we kiss, long and passionate, not caring who's watching. Not giving a damn about anything else in the world. Two people. One connection. Silverware clatters to the floor. Wine glasses tremble. Her breath is sweet. Her tongue, insatiable. And that connection of ours—a flash in time, but also a lifetime worth of passion—doesn't end 'til the wine arrives.

"Sorry," I say. "We got...carried away."

The waitress smiles, says, "No need to apologize, sir," then glides to the next customer.

"She's jealous," says Paige.

"Of what?"

"That thing we just did. The way we did it. That doesn't happen often. I can see it's never happened to her."

"That's a shame."

After we finish our wine, we take a walk. And as we walk, I talk and talk. I tell her everything, except for the shit about Lee. The untellable.

We're sitting on a bench in front of Bud Sweeny's lot, and I say, "That's everything."

"That's not everything," she says. "What about that douchebag with the sports car? That shit looked pretty serious."

I tell her about Lee, but I don't tell her about Jenny Snowdon, and this bothers me. I want to tell her everything, but how do you spill beans that hot? Answer: you don't. But the existence of such truths, they still linger in one's eyes. If she sees it, however, she's merciful. Not pressing.

I learn about her, too. She grew up in Kansas City, the Kansas side. Cody came into her life when she was fifteen. She ran from one abusive relationship to the next. Two months ago, her mom died and left her and her dad a significant amount of insurance money. Unsure what to do, they consulted with her father's accountant brother, also my business teacher from high school, Marty Sterling. He suggested they come live with him, bank the money, and figure out the future over time. Paige and her dad never had any. Money, that is. Nor time, I guess. The two, they have a way of going hand in hand. Paige and her dad decided that country living would be good for them. Good for Cody, too.

She finishes her story, then says, "Now's the time."

"What time?"

"You know my story. I know yours. So, this is it, the witching hour, when you ask me over to your place."

I consider that proposition, then, slowly, I shake my head.

"What," she says, "you don't want to?"

"I want to, but not tonight."

"Interesting."

"Don't get me wrong. I want to make love to you all night."

She puts her arm around me, moves closer, puts a hand on my thigh. "I'm listening."

"But...not tonight."

She pulls away suddenly and is still smiling despite an expression that I hope is only feigned indignation. "Tease," she says, then laughs.

"What I'm going to do is walk you home, give you the biggest goodnight kiss ever, then go home and whack off. But that's not the end, I hope. The next time you have a night off, I'm going to take you out again."

She's still laughing. "I haven't said yes yet."

"When's your next night off?"

"Tuesday."

"Wanna go out?"

"I'd love to."

This girl, I realize, could gain one hundred pounds tomorrow. All of her hair could fall out. She could lose her arms and legs. Still, I'll never see anything other than that strawberry girl walking across the street for our first date.

Grace...

She will never be anything less in my eyes.

And for the second time in my life, I know love for another human being.

SUNDAY

CHAPTER TWENTY

Tuesday is a distant memory.

And here we are—Dad, Nora, Lily, and Yours Truly. Lily's surprising us all by walking around, though the pain killers are clearly taking their toll. She occasionally excuses herself for a nap but never sleeps for more than an hour. Her spirits are remarkably high.

The past is doing what it's supposed to do. Hanging in the past.

Food keeps coming, thanks to Dad, and we keep eating.

Talking without talking. I like that notion, and I'm doing my fair share of it.

After the last dish of the day is washed, and Nora is safely tucked in bed, we take coffee onto the porch. I'm worried that without Nora things might get tense, but that fear quickly dies in the pleasant Nebraska night. We're getting another reprieve, the air actually cool. Dad and I have a splash of Kahlua in our coffee. Lily, she's just riding the meds, but she's here. Sometimes I can tell she's forcing herself here, but that's clearly because this is where she wants to be.

"I was worried this might never happen," Dad says.

Neither Lily nor I respond to this observation. We just share friendly glances filled with disbelief that this *is* happening.

"Nora's crazy about you, Dad," Lily says.

He replies, "I'm crazy about her."

Dad lights a Kool, takes a deep drag, then shakes the pack at me. I hold up a hand and say, "I'll pass."

"It's okay with me if you smoke," Lily says.

"I know," I say. "But it's not okay with Nora. Or *Paige*."

"Paige, huh?" says Dad. "So this mystery girl has a name now."

"Sound like Jacky got lucky," Lily says.

"Will we be meeting this girl soon?" asks Dad.

I respond by reaching out a hand and saying, "Okay, I'll take a smoke." And Lily and Dad laugh at me. Being the butt of the joke doesn't matter; it's just good to hear their voices joined in celebration.

I scowl, not because I'm angry, as I take a drag from the cigarette, then lean back in my chair and, letting randomness bleed past any filter, say, "Stealing night."

This gets Dad's attention. He asks, "What made you say that?"

"Just thinking about those words," I say. "You remember saying them?"

"That's what I used to tell you when oncoming cars scared you at night."

"What does it mean?" I ask.

"I don't know," he says. "A bit of poetry for a kid. Something, I guess, to help you grasp order without understanding the full truth."

"And what's the full truth?" Lily asks.

"That," Dad says, "that...sometimes the other car really is heading straight at you."

A gunshot, without warning, splits my memory wide. Again, I see Jenny Snowdon drop... The blood pooling around her head... Lee's wicked grin... And the money, all that money.

"Stealing night," I whisper.

Lily and Dad, they continue to reminisce. Lily's talking about how she used to convince me that aliens from Jupiter had killed her and taken over her body, and that she was going to kill me next. Dad and she laugh at how shitless that scared me.

New fears, however, take center stage. Fears that might fade into the wallpaper of my life, but they'll never die. Slowly, I detach from the conversation, smoking cigarette after cigarette.

Finally, Dad says, "Slow down there, Joe Camel."

"Huh?" I say.

"What's that? —your seventh?"

I cough, trying to force a smile. "Sorry," I say. "I guess I drifted on you guys."

Lily says, "'Deep Thoughts' by Jack Lewis," then she laughs.

"That's our Jack—always the deep thinker," says Dad, clearly missing the *SNL* reference.

I chuckle, pushing away dark thoughts in favor of pleasant memories, struggling to maintain purchase on the here and now.

I make my face serious and turn to my sister. "Lily," I drone.

"Yes."

"I'm not really Jack."

"Oh?"

"I'm Zebulon from the planet Jupiter..." She and Dad are already wrapped in laughter. "...and I've killed your brother and taken over his body."

"Good," she says. "I never liked my stinky brother anyway."

We're all laughing again, together, tasting freedom while far from free, and that spirit, mercifully, carries the rest of the night.

MONDAY

CHAPTER TWENTY-ONE

Bud doesn't begin the day with much discourse. Leaning back in his chair, he just smiles and says, "Lot's yours today, Jack. Work it." The cut of my suit, my clean-shaven mug—I can tell he approves of these things. What I want to talk about is money, but I don't push. Instead, I stride onto the lot and begin pacing.

One has a lot of thinking time when working a used car lot in a small town, but I don't give into darkness. I consider each of the vehicles, trying to determine who they should belong to. Sports cars are for the mid-life crisis set. SUVs are for the tough guys with families; trucks for the tough guys without families. We have a couple mini-vans, but those seem useless in Sunfall, where soccer moms are as common as poet laureates. The benefit of aspiration, however, always looms, and perhaps I'm the perfect example. So I'll keep an open mind. Ask a lot of questions. Determine who the customer wants to be before I judge who they really are. That's the ticket.

The first three hours of the day fade with no walk-ons, and that's when Bud approaches me. Flurries of fear warn of a coming storm. Fear that he'll tell me to start washing cars again. That he'll change his mind. But that's not what happens. Instead, he says, "I'm heading down to the café for a bit of lunch. Pick you up anything?"

"Chicken and provolone bagel," I say without hesitation, though I'm not really hungry. "Cucumbers, salt and pepper, mayonnaise, no tomatoes."

I reach into my pocket for money, but he stops me. "On me," he says, then gets in his sedan and drives away.

Not five minutes after he leaves, a rusty Ford truck rattles onto the lot. Looks like it might have been red once upon a time, and I don't think much of it until I notice who's in the passenger seat. My strawberry girl.

A smile more powerful than a thousand suns lights her face, and my heart soars. The guy driving has gray hair and severe lines that scream hard living from his face. This, I immediately recognize, is her dad.

She greets me with a hug; her dad with a handshake. Firm. No nonsense.

"It's good to meet you, sir," I say.

"You the guy that brought my angel home before the sun?" he growls.

"Guilty as charged," I say, wilting a little under the man's imposing presence.

His grips loosens as a grin cracks his John Wayne façade. "Good to meet you, too," he says, and I can tell he means it. "Paige here bent my ear about you all of yesterday; couldn't talk 'bout nothin' else."

I smile at her, then turn back to him. "Feeling's mutual."

"Let me cut to the chase so we don't eat up too much of your time," he says. "We're in the market, my little girl and I, for a couple of cars. I think it's high time we both have something nice to drive. Think you can help us?"

An interesting thing I learn as I'm selling Paige's father a 2006 Ford Explorer is that his name is Jack, too. That's a detail she left out, and some guys would analyze the death out of shit like that. Me, I don't care. So his name's Jack. If that helped me get my foot in the door with her, made her trust me that much more, I'm fine with it.

Paige, of all things, selects the car that Rick Mitchell had coveted, the Tiburon, and I'm happy I saved it for her.

Just in time, Bud returns. The deals are cash, and I don't know how to pull the titles. As Bud and Jack Sterling finish the exchange, Paige and I step outside.

"You should have let me give you a deal," I say.

"No," she says. "We have the money, Jack, and we're done with deals."

"As long as you don't forget I offered."

"I appreciate that. Besides, we've been talking about buying cars forever. Like Dad said, we've never had anything so nice. Cars just seemed like a good place to start."

"If you have any problems with either one, just let me know. We'll make it right."

"I know." She steps close to me and puts her arms around my shoulders. I put my arms around her waist.

Looking up at me, all eyes, she says, "So, are we like…a thing now?"

I respond with a deep but gentle kiss, then say, "Is that why you bought two cars from me? So we'd be a thing?"

"No," she laughs, then slaps me on the chest. "But I do love my new car. So cute."

"I'm glad."

"You'd better be."

"When does your shift start?"

"Two."

"Nora and I will stop by for ice cream."

"That sounds great."

"Where's Cody?"

"With his uncle."

"Uncles: the new daycare."

"Very funny," she says. "So…you didn't answer my question."

"Yeah," I say, "we're a thing."

"So, you'll stay for a while?"

And that decides me. "Wild horses couldn't drag me away, Strawberry." This is the first time I've tested the nickname on her, and I'm anxious for her reaction.

Her smile widens. "You picked a name for me?"

"Is it okay?"

"It's…" Tears cloud her eyes.

"If you don't like it—"

"I love it," she says, then kisses me. The kiss, that masterpiece kiss, it lasts long past the point of public decency, but we don't care. Here I am, praying to a god I'm starting to believe in. Praying the kiss will never end.

Her taste still on my mouth, I sit across from Bud. He's smiling wide, wider than I've ever seen.

"You're a natural," he says.

As he starts writing in a ledger, I say, "Thanks."

Not looking up, still writing, he says, "I'm only doing this once, but it's a deal you can't refuse." Then he rips something away from the ledger; a check, I realize. He hands it to me, then says, "That's every cent of profit from your three sales."

The amount staring at me: $6,723.

"Jesus Christ, Bud," is all I can say.

"He's got nothing to do with it."

"This is...this is too generous."

Bud shakes his head. "Don't ever turn down a man's courtesy, Jack. Not a commodity you're likely to encounter too damn often."

"Now," he says, "you have a choice. You can cash that check, put it with the money you saved already, and skip town. No bad feelings if you go that route. Or you can come to work for me on a fifty-fifty basis. I need to retire while I still have some miles left on my engine, and you need a career, a way to take care of that girl of yours."

"Yes," I say.

We stand, shake, then Bud says, "Do I even need to ask which option you're agreeing to?"

"No," I say, "I'm all yours."

He laughs. "Looked to me like you already belong to someone else."

"Sorry about that." I'm talking about earlier, when Bud walked up on me and Paige getting a little...hot and heavy.

"Nah," he says, "don't ever apologize for love, son. Love's the only thing worth doing this shit for."

"Amen to that," I say.

"Besides, this lot needs fresh blood. Needs children running around, too. Hell, this whole town needs more of that."

CHAPTER TWENTY-TWO

Earlier today, I took a break from work to open an account at First Confederated. Two, actually. Half the money went into savings; the other half, a college fund for Nora. The rest of my workday brought me two maybes; solid leads with invitations for follow-up. But that was then, and I promise myself, no matter what, I'll always leave work at work. The important stuff is now, sitting outside the DQ with Nora and Paige. We're eating hot fudge sundaes.

Nora puts down her spoon and says, "Hey, Paige."

"Yes, dear."

"Do you like *The Flintstones*?"

"I do," Paige says. "So does my son, Cody."

Nora's eyes go wide, and I can almost see the wheels in her brain, working out some version of world domination.

"You'll like Cody," Paige says. "Do you want to meet him?"

"When?" Paige excitedly asks.

"How 'bout tomorrow night?" I suggest, looking at Paige. "Who says the kids can't join us for dinner?"

Paige takes a big bite and nods. Pointing her red spoon at me, still swallowing, she looks down and says, "That's a good idea, Wheels."

"Wheels?" I say.

"You have a name for me," she says, "I get one for you."

"Yeah, but *Wheels*? That's kinda—"

"I like it," Nora says. "'Cause you sell cars now."

"Listen to your niece," Paige says. "She knows a good thing."

"What's your name for Paige?" Nora asks me.

"Strawberry," Paige says with a dismissive wave.

Nora and Paige laugh, then Nora wrinkles her nose. "*Strawberry*?"

"I like it," Paige says. "It's cute, don't you think?"

"Like too cute," says Nora.

We go back to eating, silent for a moment, then Nora snaps her fingers like a magician. "Hey, I've got an idea?" She turns to Paige. "What time are you done with work?"

"Eight."

"Eight's great," Nora says, throwing her attention at me. "Uncle Jack, what if Paige and Cody come over to Grandpa's...*tonight*? Just for a little while. We could watch *The Flintstones*, the Princestone one. That way your date doesn't have to be all messed up by kids."

I think about it for a moment. Not the worst idea, I'll admit.

"Grandpa wants to meet *Strawberry* anyway," Nora adds. "And it's still summer, so no school tomorrow or nothing. What do you say, Uncle Jack?"

"Yeah," Paige says, "what do you say, *Uncle Jack*?"

I point my spoon at Paige and playfully, raising my brow, say, "Thought I told you not to call me that?"

With an innocent shrug, she puts her spoon in her mouth and crosses her eyes.

Nora's lost in laughter.

"You like that idea?" I ask Paige.

"Works for me," she says. "Long as I can get Cody home by ten."

Nora slaps her hands down on the patio table with a *clang*. "So," she says, "it's settled then."

Paige leans into me. "Smart kid," she whispers.

"My dad calls her Professor."

A kiss on the cheek, then, "What do you call her?"

"Bear."

Paige takes Nora's measure for a minute, and Nora stares back with a look of righteous contentment. "Yep," Paige says, "that works, too."

As a family starts toward the order window, Paige gets up and kisses me again on the cheek. "Duty calls," she says. Then she kisses Nora on the cheek, and I'm surprised when Nora doesn't wipe it away.

Once Paige is behind the window, taking an order from a surly oaf who's trying to herd a raucous trio of monkey-children, I ask, "Do you like her?"

Nora throws her empty cup at a nearby trashcan. The cup doesn't even come close, clattering upon the shimmering asphalt. "So much for that NBA contract," she says.

When I repeat my question, Nora grips her chin and squints. "What do you think?" she growls. Nora tries, but she's a terrible actor.

"I think you do."

With a smile, she says, "Yeah, she's pretty much amazing."

CHAPTER TWENTY-THREE

We're walking to my apartment—Nora insists on picking up her *Flintstones* DVD—when we run across the black dog. On his back, belly exposed, the thing's sex is no longer a mystery. Now *he's* dead for real, covered in blood.

"Poor thing," Nora says, crouching for a closer look.

"Don't touch it," I warn.

"Why would I touch it?"

"I don't know. Just don't." I'm shocked by the sudden anger in my voice.

"Bet it was hit by a car," she whispers.

Flies circle the carcass, and I don't like her swarming with them, so I take her hand and lead her up, into cleaner air. Back where she belongs.

She's a cloud of confusion, and I don't know what to say next. So I say, "I know that dog."

"You *know* that dog?"

"I...I've fed him."

"So, are you sad? Did you *like* him?"

Heaving a sigh, I look away from her. "He's just a dog. An animal."

"Someone must have loved him once."

"You're probably right."

"But...but not enough."

"Why do you say that?"

"'Cause," she says, "they let this happen."

Taped on my front door is the latest from the landlord. An eviction notice.

"Does it say you're a wiggly worm?" Nora asks, smiling.

Shoving the folded notification in my pocket, I chuckle dryly. "Something like that." I unlock the deadbolt, push into the apartment, and Nora runs for the TV. Closing the door behind me, I say, "Hurry up," consumed by a sudden and inexplicable bout of anxiety. My eyes burn. My heart races. But Nora, she's just looking through her collection, trying to find the right disc.

Shhhuck, shhhuck, shhhuck.

Then it happens.

A shadow moves in front of me. I smell booze and Lee's nose-splitting cologne. And I feel hard steel pressed against my neck.

CHAPTER TWENTY-FOUR

Like so many times before, Lee's pacing holes in my shag carpet. But this is so very different. One, Lee's wielding a gun, waving it around. Two, and most importantly, Nora's here.

This time, he proudly informs me, the door came open with a credit card. "You did a shitty job fixing it, amigo," he accuses, pointing his gun at the door. But what can I say? When a madman divorces reason, there's no sense arguing. When they're waving a gun around the most important person in your life, a child no less, that futile notion reduces to ruble.

Nora cries and shakes, clutching my arm for salvation. She needs me now, more than ever, but that's going to change. No matter what happens, there's no avoiding the truth. No going back. She's seen my secret room, my dirty sheets.

"You're probably wondering why I came back?" Lee says.

I affirm this dark curiosity with a slow nod, pulling Nora as close and far behind me on the couch as possible.

"I vowed," Lee hisses, "never to let anyone make me feel foolish again. Never to control me, make me feel small. Feel...*wrong*. Does that make me a *baaaaad* man?"

He's a bad man, and it has nothing to do with some ridiculous vow. I want to tell him this, but I don't. I can't. Instead I say, "Put down the gun, Lee. Let Nora go. If you want to kill me, fine. Kill me. But let her run."

This intensifies Nora's shaking.

Lee studies her, one hand on his chin, the other gripping the gun that's pointed at my head. "No," he says. "Her eyes are...they're making me feel weak." Keeping the gun in my face, Lee reaches into his pocket, fishes out a wrapped piece of candy, throws it at Nora. Nora's sobs intensify.

"See," Lee says, "you give kids candy—they're supposed to like candy, aren't they?—and still they...they give you shit."

"Put the gun away," I repeat. "Let's talk."

"Done talking," Lee says. "You know what I want to do right now?"

Another slow shake of my head.

Lee's eyes, darker than midnight, press into mine. The stench of his booze-soaked breath in my face. "I want," he growls, "to take a ride."

Unable to let this madness continue, I leap at him, metal digging into my solar plexus, and we topple. Down...down...to the floor. His eyes are wide. My hands are around his neck. But the gun? Where's the gun?

A blast answers, and the pain of a thousand exploding suns blazes trails through my core. My breathing ragged.

My pulse in a race it can't win. And still my hands, they're clutching his neck. Harder...harder...every ounce of energy flowing through my hands.

Nora wails.

Lee chokes. Gasps. Chokes again. And something thumps. The gun?

I beat his head against the floor. Hard. Spots multiply. I can't breathe. Beat his head again. Harder. Harder.

Nora screams.

Tears fill my vision, everything going hazy.

And still, I pound his head. Not as hard. I don't have the strength. I can't feel my arms. I can't feel anything, and that, thankfully, includes Lee's pulse.

I fall...I fall...I fall...

In and out...

The darkest dark...The most blinding light...

Nora's fists pound my back. Screams for me to wake.

In and out...

Police sirens wail. Red and blue dances on dirty curtains.

"Uncle Jack!"

Paige and Cody are on Dad's doorstep right about now.

"Uncle Jack!"

I'm sorry, Dad. I love you.

Sorry, Strawberry. My darkness won. Sorry to be nothing more than another disappointment.

"Uncle Jack!"

Sorry, Bear. Uncle Jack's so very sorry. Loves you so very much. Of everyone, you should know that most of all. I have regrets, too many to count, but loving you is my one good thing.

My one good thing.

My throat fills with blood. I'm drowning.

And here I am, Jack Lewis, finally leaving Sunfall.

Only now, I don't want to go. I don't want to go. *I don't...*

CHAPTER TWENTY-FIVE

In a white room, I wake from darkness. Dull pain throbs, my head swimming, and someone holds my hand. No strength to move my head, I flick my eyes to the angel at my side.

"You're awake," Lily says.

"Where's Nora?" I wheeze, my throat sandpaper dry.

"She's with Dad and Paige. She's..." Tears cloud Lily's eyes. "Nora's shaken, but...she's going to be fine, thanks to you."

"I..."

"She told us how you saved her. Told the police, too. They'll want to talk to you, but everything's going to be fine, Jack. I promise."

"Lee?"

"Dead. Where he belongs."

"I...I fucked up, Lil."

"I know," she whispers. "Let's let that be our little secret, okay?"

"But I fucked up so bad."

"It won't happen again. I know it won't happen again. Besides, you've given me more than my share of second chances. Now I'm clean, Jack. Really clean, and I'm going to stay this way."

"I put Nora in danger."

"Let it go. You didn't mean to—"

"I have money, Lil," I gasp, senses fading, darkness creeping in. "You and Nora can run...run away. Get her away from me. I...I'm cursed."

Sobbing, Lily shakes her head. Then she kisses my cheek and whispers something in my ear.

"Sometimes," she whispers, "sometimes it's better not to run."

FOUR YEARS LATER

EPILOGUE

There was a time when I had nothing to live for, nothing worth dying for, no one to love, nothing to lose.

That's all changed.

Occasionally I wake from a distant dream, my old wound screaming as I gasp—no more cigarettes for One-Lung Lewis—with Jenny Snowdon's ghost haunting the cellar of my mind. But night terrors visit less and less as the world keeps turning, and Paige is always beside me for comfort. Kissing away pain.

Dad died last year. Brain cancer. Inoperable. We were all by his side when he went. I've heard it said that there's never any dignity in death. To those who buy that shit, I say, you didn't watch Charles Lewis go. The speech center of his brain was so torn up that he couldn't say goodbye with words, but his eyes did a fine job. All of us took turns letting him go, letting him know how much we loved him, and how sorry we were for wasted time.

Lily and Nora moved to Omaha last year. I still see them once or twice a month when they come to my famous customer appreciation barbecues with Lily's husband, Kyle Conrad. Kyle owns the clearinghouse that supplies much of my inventory. Paige and I—though I have to give her most of the credit—set them up on their first date. He's a good man. A good husband. And a good father. Nora's crazy about him, but me and Bear, we still have a connection.

Always will.

Paige and I have been trying to have a child. So far, no dice, but the "practicing," as she calls it, sure is fun. Anyway, the kid we already have, Cody, is handful enough. He eats us out of house and home and is starting to look like he might have a future in pro football. I take him fishing on the weekends, and we play catch in the backyard every evening. Cody *Lewis*. He took my name, calls me "Daddy," and I call him son, because he is.

We live in the house where I grew up. At first I thought of selling the place, but Paige had another idea. She said that a new generation of Lewis's should be given a chance to get it right in this house, to exorcise the past, to make it a home. I'll say this about my Strawberry Girl: she's smarter than anyone I know.

Every day the place feels a little warmer.

With Dad's help, using part of my old college fund, I bought the lot from Bud Sweeny two years ago. Business is pretty solid, people coming in from all over the county to buy my cars. I've even had customers from out of state. All right, one, and he came from northern Kansas, which isn't exactly that far away. Still, Bud swears he never had an out of state sale in all his years.

Bud and I have grown close. He enjoys retirement, but fills his empty time by working for the Sunfall Chamber of

Commerce, of which I'm president and founder. According to our records, the town actually grew by one hundred and forty-three souls last year. That number will seem paltry to city folks, but it means a hell of a lot here. A new factory went in a year and a half ago, and a new school is currently under construction.

The future sure looks brighter than the past.

Speaking of the past, the Snowdon money, even after all the talk of hiding it, was found in the trunk of Lee's car, and the case was closed. I never told anyone that I witnessed her murder, and I don't know if I ever will. In the end, I guess, we all have a dark secret, something that would extinguish all light if revealed. Guilt will always linger, judge me in the darkness, threaten me with its ugliness, and remind me…remind me that when the gun came out, I took a step back.

A step away from conflict. Me, ready to run.

Then I remind myself, I was only a child. A newborn. Since that time, I've learned so very much. I've learned to be an anchor in the storm for others. To be sturdy. And so I swallow my guilt, because it's my burden, not theirs, and I don't have time for the paradoxes of morality. I'm happy enough just being on the side of the angels.

When the Snowdons offered me the two hundred-fifty large, essentially for killing their daughter's murderer, I turned it down. They used the money instead to found an organization committed to improving the lives of mentally ill children.

Jennifer Snowdon, it turns out, was bipolar, and in love with a boy her rich parents didn't approve of, Jason Shapiro. The money that ultimately drove Lee to kill her was stolen from the family. Money for a new life.

Crazy?

Maybe.

But when her voice haunts me, when I hear her call Jason's name, I hear love, not insanity. Some will argue that love's its own form of insanity. Fuck them. I hope Jason loved her, too. I hope they're somewhere nice.

Meanwhile, the world keeps turning, and here I am, awake to feel her.

If I have my way, I'll never sleep again.

Peter Giglio
October 1, 2012
Lincoln, Nebraska

FROM SUNFALL
WITH LOVE

A special debt of gratitude is owed to my talented beta-readers for *Stealing Night*.

Eric Shaprio, one of my brothers from another mother—you always cut to the quick. Your notes on the outline and the first draft made me bleed in necessary and invaluable ways. Much love, brother.

Shannon Michaels and Bryan Walker—much gratitude from the bottom of my heart. Friendship is rare. Insightful and honest friendship is golden. Thanks for setting the gold standard so high by helping push this work to the next level.

(Note: Shortly after *Stealing Night* was accepted for publication by Nightscape Press, Bryan Walker passed away unexpectedly. A good man taken too soon. He will be missed.)

And to those who have been supportive in one way or another over the last year: Scott Bradley (my brilliant writing partner and another brother from another mother), Joe McKinney, Robert Shane Wilson, Mark Scioneaux, Jennifer Wilson, Annie Melton, John Skipp, Karen Giglio, Frank Hall, Gwen Perkins, Rhoda Jordan, Ava Gerard, Gregory L. Norris, Trent Zelazny, Peter N. Dudar, Geoff Kruse, Gene O'Neill, Rick Hautala, Holly Newstein, Eric J. Guignard, Hank and Holly Snider, David Bernstein, Sandy Shelonchik, Mark Allan Gunnells, Jeremy C. Shipp, Ivana Lovric, and Charles Day. If I forgot your name, I'm sorry. The last year has brought me an embarrassment of riches and it's regrettably all-too-easy to forget every kind gesture and moment of grace.

There have been many.

Thank you.

Love,

PG